The Musings of

HE

This is a work of fiction. Names, characters, institutions, and events are either the product of the author's imagination or used fictitiously. Any resemblance to actual persons, living or dead, is entirely coincidental—though not always dismissible.

First edition

Published by Hillsather Publishing House

www.elowengreywell.com

Curated under the supervision of Benedict Lowre, Archivist Emeritus

ISBN: 979-8-9993361-1-8

Printed in the United States of America

Catalogued under: Literary Fiction, Gothic Horror, Archival Curiosities

To be handled with care. Contents may unsettle.

To Vattica, he who dragged me off the bathroom floor and told me to write.

A Caution

What you are about to read perhaps demands a preface. A warning, perhaps—or at the very least, an introduction to the world into which you now step. Beyond this page lie the unedited, and most crucially, unfiltered words of the late Vattica Wilde.

Before we descend too far, it is important that we offer context—not only of the man, but of the reason this manuscript has found its way to you.

Vattica Wilde was a Franco-British author of rare promise. A weaver of language, devoted entirely to his craft. You may know his name from the once-acclaimed novel *The Brothers of Gold*, a stirring tale of kinship and survival amidst the soot and blood of 18th-century France. A work that left London enraptured, not only for its poetry, but for the shocking realization that it was, at least in part, true.

Wilde had lived it. Or rather, survived it.

It is known, that *The Brothers of Gold*, one of the siblings does not endure, the tale steeped in agony, hunger, and human desperation. Readers found beauty in the ache, and horror in the truth. But Wilde, it seemed, was left with little more than a wound that would never truly close.

What followed that triumph was a steep and steady fall.

His subsequent works failed to captivate audiences the way his suffering once did. Publishers turned their backs, the public, ever fickle, embraced newer names and fresher voices. And Wilde—once the darling of literary London—became a footnote, a has-been, a man obsessed with rekindling a candle once held to the world.

Which brings us here.

What follows is not a novel, but a journal—discovered in its entirety under unsettling circumstances, which we shall detail in the postscripts. These are Vattica Wilde's final writings, presented as they were found, with minimal interference. In places, you will encounter facsimiles of pages that could not be translated or transcribed without losing something... vital. Something true.

Let us be clear: this is not a story of redemption.

There is no love here. No light at the end.

This is the unraveling of a man. Whether by madness or by something else entirely, we leave it to you.

You may consider these pages as a spiritual document. Or as the ravings of a deluded mind. But know this: the horrors detailed herein are no mere inventions of literary craft. Something happened within the walls of that manor. Something only Wilde ever truly saw.

And whether he glimpsed the divine, the damned, or only himself, we cannot say.

But he wrote. God, he wrote.

This is, as he so feverishly desired, his magnum opus.

—Benedict Lowre
Hillsather Publishing House

"Madness, like authorship, is contagious.
And ink, once spilled, remembers everything."

From the Hillsather Folio on Unauthored Texts (Unpulished)

ENTRY I: The Literary Plague

15th of February, London, This Bleak Morning

The morning arrived draped in mist, as though Heaven itself sought to obscure the city from God's own gaze. London—that ever-choking behemoth of soot and sorrow—wheezed to life with its usual cacophony of street hawkers, carriage wheels, and the incessant whimpering of hungry dogs.

My breakfast, if one could call it that, consisted of half a biscuit and a pot of tea gone bitter from reboiling. I did not have the stomach to handle it.

No sooner had I seated myself by the window of my modest quarters—if such a title befits the draughty alcove I rent above a chandler's shop—than a letter slid itself beneath the door like a snake slithering into my life.

The envelope bore no fanfare, no embossed crest of a reputable publisher, but I knew its intent before I broke the seal. Even in its silence, the letter mocked me. I could smell its insolence.

With trembling fingers, I opened it. Its contents were no more than I anticipated: another rejection, penned in language that attempted civility but betrayed its author's disdain with every stroke.

"We thank you for your submission, Mr. Wilde, but regret to inform you that it does not suit our current publishing direction."

The nerve! The audacity! As though I—Vattica Wilde, one-time darling of the literary salons—had submitted an amateur's scribble!

Suddenly they fancy themselves arbiters of taste, while I, the true craftsman of narrative, am deemed unworthy. Regret! What know they of regret? They sit in their warm offices with their quills and ledgers, sorting through manuscripts like fishwives sifting spoiled cod.

They have become gluttons of mediocrity, vomiting out the same paltry stories into the public's eager mouth, all while sneering at anything bearing the scent of originality.

They claim my work lacks "modern appeal." I ask: What is modern appeal if not another phrase for intellectual cowardice? I gave them a tale filled with fire and blood, and they craved lukewarm broth!

The very same structures—the same artifice and cadence that once birthed *The Brothers of Gold*, the novel that made London weep and women swoon in tea parlours—are now considered "too overwrought." "Too lyrical." "Too dense."

They would rather publish the empty scribblings of some foppish dandy writing about spoiled heiresses at garden parties.

My former publisher, Wexley & Sons, dared drop me as one might drop spoiled fruit—too soon and with great disdain. Their letter of dismissal was curt, almost offended in its brevity.

"We must regrettably cease our professional relationship, effective immediately."

No explanation. No farewell. No fond remembrance of the revenues I once brought them, nor the accolades they so proudly emblazoned across their catalogues.

Was I not once the voice of a generation? Did I not dine with critics who toasted to my genius with vintage port and whispered my name with reverence?

And now? Now I am cast aside like a molted skin, irrelevant to a world that has fattened itself on frivolity. Even my so-called acquaintances have begun to drift like smoke in the winter air. One by one, their invitations dwindled, their correspondence growing dry, infrequent, brittle with pleasantry.

I am becoming a ghost, haunting the very streets I once graced.

There are days I wonder if it is I who have changed. Perhaps the city is the same, and it is my own mind that has rotted beneath the weight of unmet expectations and unfulfilled promises.

I stare for hours at the blank pages stacked upon my desk, and they, like cruel mirrors, reflect not inspiration but absence—an echoing void where once there resided lightning. The muses, it seems, have abandoned me.

The rent is due in a week. The firewood dwindles. My ink is thick with cold.

And still, I write.

I write because I must, though I feel each word drips not from my pen but from some cracked portion of my soul. I write as the condemned man chants his final prayer. Not in hope, but from sheer compulsion.

And then there is the dripping.

Yes. The dripping.

It began three nights ago. A steady, rhythmic tapping that seems to originate from somewhere within the wall behind my bed.

I have examined the plaster, searched for leaks, and checked the eaves. Nothing. No sign of moisture, no loose pipe, no nest of rodents gnawing at the timbers.

And yet, each night, just as the lamps are dimmed and the air turns still, the sound begins.

Drip. Drip. Drip.

Not constant. Not rushed.

But deliberate. Measured.

As though *something* thinks before each drop.

I attempted to ignore it at first—a trick of the house, I thought. A symptom of age and winter damp. But now, it finds its way into my dreams.

I awaken with the sound pressing against my skull, a metronome for some infernal composition.

I rise.

Check the room.

Find nothing.

And lie awake until morning, staring at the ceiling as my thoughts rot like meat.

Perhaps, it is a sign. A portent. A whisper from some hidden place beneath my floorboards.

Or perhaps I am merely slipping—like my career, like the city's fog—into obscurity.

Regardless, I feel something must change.

I am not a man content to be forgotten.

If London has no place for Vattica Wilde, then let the provinces tremble. Let the moors echo with prose.

I have heard rumors—strange, vague mutterings of a manor far from the smoke. Empty for years. Owned by no one, and yet always spoken of as though it waits.

I shall make enquiries.

I need quiet. Solitude. A place where the muses might once again alight upon my shoulder, if only to whisper farewell.

Should I find this house, I shall write there.

I shall resurrect myself.

Or die trying.

But for now, the ink runs dry. And the room grows cold.

And still...

Drip.

Drip.

Drip.

—Vattica Wilde

ENTRY II: Soot and Spectacles

17th of February, London, Horrid Day

I was awoken this morning by the most ghastly of sounds—the dripping.

A maddening, ceaseless drip from the ceiling near my hearth. It echoed like the ticking of some infernal clock, intent on counting down my final moments of sanity!

I sat upright in bed, the grey light of dawn crawling like a wounded beast across the warped floorboards of my lodging.

I stared at the corner where the leak persisted, waiting for it to still itself as it so often does in the presence of others.

But it did not.

Not today.

Today, it mocked me.

I rose from bed, my joints aching with a stiffness most unbecoming of a man not yet past his prime. With robe and slippers hastily donned, I made my way to the corridor. It was as cold as the devil's breath, and my own rose in plumes before me.

I swore under it, for even my exhalations are nobler than the rodents that skitter below my floorboards.

I pounded upon the landlord's door with the fury of Caesar betrayed.

The man—a rotund, slovenly figure with the pallor of spoiled milk and the scent of worse whisky—answered in a red and white striped nightshirt, his nose as red as his shame ought to have been.

I could not resist wrinkling my nose in disgust. His apartment reeks of whores. That sticky-sweet scent of off perfume, sweat, and desperation.

I despise that smell.

I despise whores.

I told him, in no uncertain terms, that the dripping had persisted and must be attended to with immediate urgency.

He stared at me, eyes half-lidded and mind most certainly absent, and muttered something to the effect of "no drip to be heard."

The gall!

I insisted again, louder this time, and he made a great show of rubbing sleep from his face before trailing after me like an obedient sow.

But lo! When we entered the flat, the dripping had ceased.

Utter silence.

I stood aghast, my finger raised toward the spot from whence the drip had most certainly emanated. But there was nothing.

He stood behind me, arms crossed, breath hot and rank against the back of my neck.

"You see?" he grunted, as though he had won some great philosophical debate. "Told you there weren't no sound. You writers are always hearin' things."

My blood boiled.

I turned to offer him a mouthful of righteous indignation, but he had already vanished.

I swear upon all that is holy, he had been behind me not a breath before, and yet now—nothing.

No creak of retreating floorboards. No slam of the door.

Only silence, and the faint aroma of unwashed flesh.

I rushed to the hallway and scanned in either direction. Empty. Only the distant creak of the building's bones and a faint cough echoing from the floors above.

What trickery was this?

He could not have moved so swiftly. He is not a spry man, not in the least.

To call him "fleet of foot" would be to insult the very concept of movement.

He is heavy, ponderous—a man with the gait of a stuffed sofa.

And yet, he had vanished like a spectre.

A curious unease settled over me then, and I was reminded of the dream I had the night before:

A dark hallway.

A dripping sound.

A door with no handle.

And behind it... something whispering my name.

I returned to my quarters and sat at my desk, intent upon writing, but the pen refused me.

My hand shook. Trembled.

Instead, I paced. Back and forth like a caged lion in the menagerie at Hyde Park.

My thoughts would not settle. My words eluded me, as though my muse had grown weary of the cold and taken flight.

Eventually, I calmed myself with a spot of weak tea and a dry heel of bread.

No jam. No butter. Not even a slice of cheese to mock the effort.

I have fallen far from the days when I supped at private clubs and basked in the laughter of men who once called me *genius*.

Now, I sit alone in a frigid flat with peeling wallpaper and a mouse that watches me from beneath the stove as though it judges my every syllable.

When I attempted to pen another chapter of my latest manuscript, *Hearth and Gallows*—a bleak tale of betrayal and blood meant to mimic the success of *The Brothers of Gold*—I found that I could not concentrate.

Every sentence fell like dust from a crumbling shelf: lifeless and insipid.

Worse still, the dripping resumed.

By God, I nearly screamed.

But I did not. I would not give the landlord the satisfaction.

No.

I merely rose, fetched a pail from the kitchen, and placed it beneath the source of the sound.

It is an ugly thing, the pail—rusted at the rim, dented at the side.

But it does its work.

It collects the drip.

Drip.

Drip.

Drip.

It is now past midnight, and I sit here writing by candlelight.

The pail is half full.

The mouse sleeps.

The world outside is still, and the air carries the faint perfume of woodsmoke and soot.

I must escape this place.

I have begun to entertain the notion of removing myself from the city.

The filth. The noise.

The people who once lauded me, now indifferent to my very existence.

Once again, my thoughts drift to the manor, somewhere

far beyond the city's reach.

An acquaintance once spoke of it—*Hollisby*, I believe it was called. A sprawling estate left to rot after some ghastly affair, decades past.

He said it was still standing, though barely.

"A good place for ghosts," he joked.

"A fine place to go mad." I laughed at the time.

Now, I wonder if it might be precisely what I need.

A new start.

Silence.

Solitude.

And perhaps—if the spirits are kind—*inspiration*. I shall inquire about it on morrow.

—*V. Wilde*

ENTRY III: The Man in 414

18th of February, London, A Day Best Left Undone

I awoke this morning not with grace nor in comfort, but with a start—heart hammering like a war drum beneath my ribs.

A dream had wrapped itself tightly around my throat.

No memory remained of it, save the sensation of being watched—stared at from some hidden place beneath the floorboards.

It left me clammy, my eyes crusted with sweat rather than sleep, the skin of my hands trembling as I reached for the inkpot. I had half a mind to write the feeling down, but what words are there for a dread that has neither face nor cause?

The dripping had returned.

No, *returned* is the wrong word.

It had *persisted*, faithfully, like a loyal servant tending to my madness.

Drip. Drip. Drip.

Even now, I hear it as I write. That metronome of doom above my desk.

The spot in the ceiling has darkened further, bulging like a blister in the skin of this decaying house.

I asked the landlord again this afternoon—*again*—and as before, he dismissed it with a wave of his liver-spotted hand

and the patronizing patience of one speaking to an imbecile.

"There's no flat above you, Mr. Wilde," he insisted. "That's the roof. Just the roof. You're imagining things."

But I *know* the sound of water when it falls from rot.

I know the difference between a storm's leak and a persistent wetness born of something *living* in the walls.

He lies, plainly.

There is someone up there.

I hear them walk—slow, dragging steps in the middle of the night.

And this morning, when I pressed my ear to the ceiling, I heard breathing.

Breathing.

The landlord's tone bore the thinnest veil of contempt.

"If I catch you up there again, sir," he warned, "there'll be consequences. It's a sealed room. You've no business touching the hatch."

He called it *Room 414*, a number I do not recall on the building's registry.

"No such tenant," he muttered. "Just beams and black mold." But his eyes betrayed the lie.

He *knows* who—or what—is in that room.

He is frightened of it, though he dares not say why.

I am *not* mad.

I know madness.

I have seen it in poets with ink-stained hands and laughing mouths; in women who tear at the air and scream about lost children; in drunks who speak to the moon.

This is not that.

This is *clarity.*

The numbers repeat themselves now. 414 scratched on the back of a gas bill I found tucked beneath my door. Circled in charcoal on the corner of this morning's newspaper.

I saw them again in the condensation of a carriage window, the fog clearing to reveal that ghostly impression on the glass.

Coincidence is a fool's word.

Pattern is the mother of all revelation.

My writing, I admit, has suffered.

Every paragraph I produce feels clotted and sticky, like blood dried too long beneath a fingernail.

Hearth and Gallows—my poor manuscript—groans under the weight of my distracted pen.

I catch myself rewriting the same page three times, only to find that each version differs not at all.

My own prose reads like that of a stranger now: distant, cold, even cruel.

The characters speak in riddles I do not remember inventing.

I went again to the stairwell that leads to the upper level.

The landlord has affixed a crude latch over the crawl hatch at the top landing, claiming it has been sealed for "forty years or more."

Then why, I ask, are the scuff marks on the boards *fresh*?

Why does the latch creak as though it is *often* used?

And why, for God's sake, does that dripping sound come from *behind* it?

I pressed my palm against the wood.

It was *warm*.

As I turned to descend the steps, I caught a glimpse—just at the corner of my eye—of something moving in the hall below.

A shape.

Not human.

It ducked out of sight before I could properly register it, but the impression remains: a tall figure, wrapped entirely in shadow, gliding as if weightless across the floor.

I nearly called out, but found my tongue held hostage by fear.

I returned to my room in silence and locked the door.

I have begun to doubt my own senses.

This evening, over the noise of the city and the crackle of my lamp, I heard a knock at the wall.

Not the door—the *wall*.

Three taps, deliberate, from the direction of Room 414.

I pressed my ear to it, and after a moment of stillness, a voice followed—thin, rasping, as though filtered through many layers of gauze.

"You hear it too."

I pulled back, breath catching in my throat.

There was nothing more.

I write now with shaking fingers, my candle guttering in its dish.

The room feels colder than it ought.

My coat, draped over the chair across from me, moved—just slightly—as though someone had brushed past it.

I refuse to believe this is madness. There is a design to it all.

The landlord is hiding something.

Room 414 exists.

And there is someone in it who wishes to speak with me.

Not some ghost, nor hallucination—no.

Something far older and darker, carved from the marrow of the world.

If I were mad, I would be *comforted*.

But this is real.

414.

415.

416.

— *V. Wilde*

ENTRY IV: Inquiring Minds

18th of February, London Midday

I have made enquiries. The manor exists.

It is not some fanciful conjuration of a desperate mind, nor an idle tale spun over claret in smoke-filled parlours. *Hollisby Manor*, as it is properly named, is very real—though little spoken of these days. I visited an old friend—Mr. Reginald Penworthy— who now resides on the edge of Chiswick, in a house cluttered with faded maps and relics from Egypt, where once he fancied himself an explorer of tombs and truths better left buried.

Reginald, though aged and prone to flights of grandiose memory, retains a mind sharp as a bodkin when it comes to such matters. I had barely uttered the name before he stiffened, as though I had spoken some long-forbidden invocation.

"Hollisby?" he asked, voice hoarse with dust. "You mean to say you're going there?"

"I mean to consider it," I replied, folding my gloved hands over my cane. "A place of quiet. A retreat. London no longer suits me."

He poured us both a measure of brandy, his hands trembling with something that felt like more than age.

"It's cursed," he muttered.

Naturally, I scoffed, though inwardly, I admit I relished the drama of it.

"Cursed," I repeated with the faintest smile. "In what fashion, precisely? Haunted? Hexed by witches? Or merely beset by bad plumbing and the usual English gloom?"

He did not smile in return.

"They say the last inhabitant vanished," he said. "Not died— vanished. No body, no farewell, not a trace left behind save his journals. And those were... unreadable. Mad. Riddled with ink blots and nonsensical ramblings. He wrote of voices in the walls, shadows that moved against the grain of light, and doors that changed places when no one watched."

This piqued my interest.

"What year was this?" I asked, too quickly.

"God, I don't recall. Perhaps fifty years past. Perhaps longer. The estate fell into disrepair shortly after, and no one has lived there since. The village nearby refuses to go near it. Even the farmers won't let their sheep graze near the hedges."

I thanked him with all due civility and took my leave, though he begged me in a half-serious tone to reconsider.

"Go to Bath instead," he offered. "The waters do wonders for the nerves."

But I am not a man of waters. I am a man of words. Of ink and shadow. *Hollisby* calls to me not with the promise of rest, but of relevance.

There is something there—I feel it. Something that may inspire me once more, shake me from this ceaseless creative decay.

And yet, as I write this, a strange sensation lingers in my chest—not fear, no. Not precisely. But a sense of premonition, as though I have already crossed a threshold I cannot uncross. Even now, as the candlelight flickers upon my wall, the shadows seem longer than they ought. The very air feels heavier, as though thickened by thought.

I dreamt again last night.

This time, I walked the halls of a great house. Empty, save for paintings with no faces and clocks with no hands. There was a door at the end of a long corridor—black, wooden, ancient. And behind it, something waited. Not menacing. Not even malevolent. But aware. And hungry.

I awoke with blood in my nose.

The bleeding has stopped now, and I feel mostly well. The physician says it is nothing—a touch of dryness, or perhaps nerves. I did not mention the dreams. Nor the dripping, which has returned with renewed vigour. I hear it now, as I write— steady as a funeral drum.

Drip. Drip. Drip.

I shall take it as a sign.

I have penned a letter to the solicitor who manages the Hollisby estate—Mr. Ashcroft, a name that appears to belong to no living man, according to my landlord, but which I found listed in the back pages of a battered registry.

The letter shall go out in the morning with the first post.

I have requested visitation.

If the house accepts me, I shall depart within the month. Something tells me I must.

— *V. Wilde*

ENTRY V: Rats in the Walls

20th of February, London, In the Company of Vermin

/ / /

I awoke to scratching.

Not outside, nor underfoot, but within the very walls themselves. A rustling, a nesting, a sound suggesting teeth and claw. The slow, deliberate erosion of wood and sanity alike. I sat upright, breath caught in my throat, and the moment I stilled to listen, it ceased. Not silence, no. But that *kind* of silence that has shape and weight. The kind that watches.

I know now there are rats in the walls.

No one believes me, of course. Not the landlord. Not the man with the opium cart in the alley. Not even the blind priest who nods politely and crosses himself as I pass. "It's London," they say. "All walls have rats."

But these are not city rats. Not the filthy grey wretches that crawl through the bones of this metropolis in search of bread crusts and drunken toes. These *speak*. Not in words, but in something older, something that hums behind the ear. A language felt, not heard. A whisper just below meaning. They do not scurry—they *pace*.

And they know my name.

It began two nights ago. The dripping had finally stopped. Vanished. And a beautiful silence bloomed in its absence— as if the ceiling itself were holding its breath. And then, that sound—*skritch-skritch-skritch*—from inside the panel behind my bookshelf. I approached it cautiously, laying my ear against the flowered paper. What I heard, I shall never unhear:

A voice. Not spoken aloud, not truly. But pressed into my mind like a thumbprint into wax.

"*You are the seed,*" it breathed. "*Watered by worms. Grown in rot.*"

I reeled back, nearly falling over my chair.

I stayed awake until the grey hours, long past the point when dreams blur into memory. When I finally slept, I dreamt of teeth—countless white knives buried in dark fur, chittering in rhythm. I stood ankle-deep in them, the rats. They churned around my feet, tails wrapping my legs like cords, dragging me downward.

And above me, on the landing where the attic hatch should be, stood the figure again—tall, draped in shadow, hands folded behind his back like a patient host. His face was a void. A mask made of night. And from the hollows where his eyes should be, I saw myself reflected—mouth open, screaming without sound.

I awoke with the taste of copper.

The number repeats itself again—414—etched in frost upon my windowpane this morning. I watched it melt, its edges curling like dying paper. I tried to ignore it, distract myself, busy my hands with writing. But the story has grown wrong. *Hearth and Gallows* bends in new directions, reshaping itself against my will. The protagonist, once a noble outcast, now mutters blasphemies I never penned. The gallows has become a throne. The hearth—an altar.

The manuscript lives now. It bleeds ink when I press too hard.

The gaslight sputters when I write its title.

I heard the rats again at dusk. Louder now. Closer. I pounded the walls, shouted threats, and for one breathless second, they fell silent. And then came laughter—not human. A sound made by *many* mouths. High-pitched. Rasping. As if dozens of throats gurgled joy at my expense.

I cannot think. I cannot breathe without hearing them. Even now, as I write, I catch glimpses of movement from the corners of my eyes. The floorboards bulge. My boots scrape against symbols I don't remember carving.

I opened a floorboard this morning. Just one.

Nothing inside. No nest. No rat droppings. But the smell—like damp parchment and old fur and something *sweet* underneath it. I reached in and pulled out a scrap of cloth. Black. Filthy. Writhing with tiny holes like the cloth had been *breathed through*.

414.

It pulses now, that number. Like a heartbeat in the paper. It wakes me in the middle of the night, draws itself on the mirror while I shave. I write it without meaning to—on napkins, in book margins, even on the inside of my wrist.

The landlord appeared again today, his mood clipped and acidic. He brought with him a young woman, thin and pale as a church candle. "She's here to clean," he said. "Says she can help with your… condition."

She watched me from the corner of her eye as she scrubbed at my walls. Not a speck of dust disturbed, and yet she wiped and wiped and wiped. I asked her if she'd ever been to the attic.

She stopped mid-motion. Stared. "There's no attic," she

whispered.

I asked her what was above me, then.

She didn't answer. She left soon after. She did not touch the doorknob as she left.

The walls are bleeding now—not visibly, not to others, but I *feel* it. Cold drafts seep from beneath the floor. My books smell like a butcher's apron. The voice returned last night, but this time it said something else:

"*It gnaws, Vattica. It* gnaws *you from the inside.*"

I think I'm beginning to understand what it means.

But here's the strangest thing of all: I'm no longer frightened. I am *angry*. That such filth crawls behind my walls. That I am spoken to in riddles by rats and shadows. That I must tiptoe through my own thoughts for fear they are *his*.

I went to the base of the stairs today and stared up at the hatch again.

There were scratches around it. Long ones.

Claw marks.

I believe the thing in Room 414 is no longer content to whisper.

I believe it intends to come down. And I will be waiting.

— *V. Wilde*

ENTRY VI: The Fall from Grace

22nd of February, London, In Her Final Embrace

Today, I did the unthinkable:

I set down my pen.

Not in defeat—no, never that—but in exhaustion. There is a distinction, I think. The novelist's greatest tool is not the pen, nor even the hand that guides it, but the mind that sharpens it. And mine—God help me—has grown as dull as a butcher's block of late.

So, I did what any self-respecting madman might do when words abandon him: I took a walk.

I descended from my attic chamber, the very walls groaning as though mourning my absence, and stepped into the airless murk of the London morning. The city stank of horse piss and coal smoke, yet something about it felt almost romantic today. Or perhaps, I merely *chose* to see it as such. There is a certain sickness in nostalgia, is there not?

Market Street greeted me with her usual din. Hawkers barking about turnips, pamphleteers screaming salvation, gutters running black.

But what caught my eye—no, my ego—was the absence of recognition.

Once, I could not walk these streets without being accosted for a signature or a sermon. Once, the name *Vattica Wilde* was passed like communion bread among the hopeful and the literate. But today? Today, I was nothing more than a waif in a threadbare coat.

A few smiles and nods as a baker woman asked after the next volume of *The Brothers of Gold*. That almost pulled a smile from me. Almost. A faint tug at the corner of my mouth—like a fishhook beneath the skin. But it faded just as swiftly. Nostalgia again.

Still, the fresh air—if one can call the London miasma

"*fresh*,,—seeped into me like opium. I walked further than intended. Past the butchers. Past the old bookshop where they once displayed my novel in the window. Past that pitiful alley where I once watched a poet retch gin onto his boots while reciting Wordsworth.

I walked until I found myself before the church.

It was not intentional, I assure you. I do not go to churches. Not for years. Not since boyhood. Yet there it was, brick and stone and silence. The old wooden doors sat slightly ajar—like the maw of something ancient and kind.

And I, fool that I am, entered.

The light within was dim, what little of it filtered through stained-glass eyes and haloes. There were only a few others: two elderly women murmuring prayers in fractured Latin, and a man in a black coat slouched like a corpse in the rear pew.

I did not pray. I do not pray.

Perhaps in my childhood I would be the sort to diligently fall to his knees and beg the sky for remission.

I wonder who taught me such a thing. Who would teach a child to make wishes on things other than stars and beg a nonexistent voice for favours? How shameful.

36

Regardless, I did not pray.

But I did sit.

The pew welcomed me like an old friend. The scent of wax and age was comforting, in its way. And before me stood a statue of the Virgin Mary, hands clasped delicately, gaze cast downward. What love was carved into her marble expression— what gentle mourning, as if she too had lost something irreplaceable.

I hold no disdain for art, the creation of stories without words. Perhaps that is why I did not despise the figure. She was silent (she was made of stone, after all) but her eyes conveyed a deep love.

Love for a martyr.

It made me sick.

Not from blasphemy, no—I've never been one for petty rebellion. But from a deeper place, a child's place. For as I gazed upon her stone face, the question rose in my mind like bile: Who taught her to fold her hands and pray?

Who taught *any* of us to fold and beg? To petition the air? To ask the empty heavens for something we do not deserve?

I stood then. Abruptly. A chill gnawed at my spine, and I could not bear the quiet judgment of her sculpted gaze.

In that moment I decided I had quite enough of Mary and her martyr and bowed heads and folded hands. I stood and saw myself out.

Swiftly. Almost... desperately.

And then I ran.

Why did I run?

Why was I running?

Even now, I cannot tell you. I remember only the sensation of being watched. Not by the statue—no, she was innocent in her stone—but by *something*. Something I could not name.

My boots pounded the cobblestones like war drums. I ran past the bakers, the butchers, the booksellers. I do not recall catching my breath. Only the fear. The certainty that something followed. The gaze of God upon a heretic.

I arrived at my building half-mad with exertion, lungs aflame, vision swimming. My coat was askew, my cravat limp with sweat. I stumbled up the stairs two at a time.

And that was when I saw it.

My possessions. My manuscripts. My trunks. All of it— tossed like refuse onto the landing. My apartment door, once stiff with neglect, now hung slightly ajar, stripped of its lock.

I stood for a long time, unable to enter.

The door creaked softly in the draught—a cruel, beckoning gesture.

I stepped forward and pushed it open.

Inside: ruin.

My bed stripped bare. The writing desk overturned. Pages scattered like carrion feathers across the floor. My ink pots smashed. The painting of my mother—gone. I fell to my knees, trembling. Whether from rage or despair, I could not say.

This was not burglary. No thief would be so *particular*.

It was eviction.

That *swine* of a landlord—the bastard—he had warned me, hadn't he? Hinted at arrears. Muttered about "sanity" and "complaints." But I thought them idle threats.

I should have known. He wanted me gone. He feared me. Feared the dripping, the strange hours, the *talking*.

Let him fear.

Let him think me mad.

I gathered what I could—my penknife, a few unspoiled pages, the silver ring I stole from a drunkard's pocket as a boy. I bundled them into my coat. I turned back one last time, and for a moment, I saw something move at the corner of the room— something blacker than shadow. But when I looked directly, there was nothing.

Of course, there was nothing.

I left that place. That coffin of a room. I descended the stairs without looking back.

And at the base of the stairs, I found the landlord waiting.

He did not speak. He only stared. I smiled at him, wide and toothless, like a corpse. And then I said:

"414."

He blinked.

I did not explain. I did not need to.

Let that number haunt him as it haunts me.

And now, here I sit in a public house, quill in hand, paper

stolen from the pubkeep's storeroom. I am drinking cheap port from a cracked glass, and I am writing you this entry.

Tomorrow, I go to Hollisby.

The manor is mine now. It cost me the last of my coin and perhaps my last thread of sense, but it is *mine*. I shall retreat into its bones, and there I shall write *Hearth and Gallows*, and it shall birth something so terrible and beautiful that the world shall *choke* on it.

Farewell, London. You clot of brick and bile. You broke me, but I shall rebuild in my own image.

And to whomever may read my words, including myself, I pray you never fold your hands and beg. Fold them instead for war.

— *V. Wilde*

ENTRY VII: Swine and Simps

22nd of February, London, My Loathsome Goodbye

I write this now from the corner of a public house that smells of boiled meat and spilt dreams. The innkeeper eyes me with suspicion—rightly so. I did not pay for the ink I stole from his ledger drawer, nor for the parchment now crumpling beneath my palm. But I offer him something better than coin: legacy. These are the last words I shall write in London.

A few hours ago, I was cast out like refuse. My manuscripts scattered. My belongings bruised. My landlord—a rodent masquerading as a man—stood at the base of the stairs like some municipal god of petty vengeance, and I—bruised of pride, not flesh—smiled and left my mark.

Let him gnaw on regret.

Even now, hours later, his face lingers in the folds of my mind like a wine stain. The bulbous nose, the sweating brow, the lips constantly moist with self-congratulation. Mr. Tupp, self-appointed keeper of my decay. I wonder if he thought himself noble in that moment. I wonder if he felt a surge of righteous deliverance as he watched me gather my belongings like a beaten dog. He would not understand what he has done. He has not rid himself of a tenant. He has created a myth.

And yet, despite my righteous fury, I find myself thinking of that awful garret. That cramped, sweating prison above the chandler's shop—a dwelling so narrow it felt more like a corridor forgotten by architecture. The ceiling sagged in places, yellowed with ancient damp, and the floor groaned like a man in prayer.

The walls would sweat in summer and freeze in winter. The air was filled with the scent of wax, coal dust, and something else I cannot name—a sweetness that rots. And the ceaseless drip above my bed.

God, the dripping. I swore it had begun to mimic speech. That it paused expectantly after every drop as if waiting for me to reply. At first I ignored it. Then I reasoned with it. Then I threatened it. Last night I shouted at it until my throat grew raw, until I wept and laughed and begged the ceiling to either collapse or be silent. It did neither.

Was that what finally drove Tupp to act? Or was it the manuscript itself—its rhythm, its appetite? The things I wrote within those walls were not kind. They were not gentle. I have seen lesser men unsettled by lesser drafts.

He suspected me of being mad, and perhaps I am. But I ask— madness in comparison to what? The man spends his days wringing rent from the near-dead and feeding slop to pigeons. He reeks of onions and failure. If I am mad, at least I am *interesting*.

He was always listening, I know that now. I caught him once, crouched at my door, his face pressed near the keyhole like a dog sniffing at carrion. He bolted when I called his name, nearly toppling down the stairs. He tried to laugh it off the next day, said he'd thought he heard rats. And in a way, he did. He heard something gnawing, but it wasn't vermin. It was me.

London has rejected me, shunned me like a sick dog. The critics, the clerks, the hollow-eyed patrons of Wexley & Sons—all of them chewed my name and spat it out. Once, they praised me. Once, they fought over my words like dogs at a butcher's block. But now? Now I am a footnote in their ledgers. A cautionary tale in half-whispered tones. "Have you heard of Wilde?" they murmur. "Terrible business. Shame about the mind."

But they know nothing of the mind. Nothing of mine.

I have outgrown this city. It no longer contains me. The fog chokes, the streets reek of urine and sanctimony, and the people—God, the people. Their eyes are dull with mediocrity. Their mouths never stop moving, mouthing borrowed opinions and recycled condemnations. Their praise means less than piss in a chamber pot.

Even the booksellers have turned. Once, my face graced the windows. Once, I watched readers clutch my novel like a rosary. But yesterday, I passed that very shop and saw a stack of gardening manuals in its place. One of them was called *The Tender Vine*. Imagine. *The Tender Vine*.

I am no vine. I am root and rot and rupture.

But I am free now. Truly.

It is a place that stifled the spirit, suffocates the imagination. No wonder my art would not bloom here. No genius could survive.

Yet I survived, barely. And now, I depart.

The decision to leave was not born in a moment, but in a thousand slow deaths. Each rejection, each insult, each missed letter, each scowl from Tupp, each failed attempt at prayer before an indifferent statue. These things do not wound, not individually. But together? Together they bury.

I have clawed my way back to breath.

Hollisby awaits. The name alone sings. It conjures ivy and smoke and mirrors covered in sheets. It is not a home. It is a cathedral of abandonment. A carcass with architecture. I have seen it in dreams. I walked its corridors barefoot. I touched its peeling wallpaper, its bannister slick with time. I stood in its hall and heard it exhale.

They say it is haunted. That no one lives there. That the floorboards cry out at night and the birds do not sing.

I say: good.

Let it be haunted. Let it creak and weep and watch me while I sleep. Let it moan and shiver and whisper in the walls. I have spoken to ceilings before. I can speak to this one, too.

The manor is mine now. Paid for in full. I drained the last of my coin, pawned the last of my jewellery—all but the silver ring I stole from that drunkard outside St. Giles. He won't miss it. He's probably dead. I hope he is. That ring has work to do.

The solicitor who sold me Hollisby laughed. He said, "Most writers want cottages, not corpses." I told him I preferred bones. They are more honest.

The coach is arranged. The driver is mute, they say. A man without language is a man without judgment. I will not be looked at. I will not be pitied. I will not be asked what I intend to do with the house.

I intend to bleed on its floors.

Let Tupp gossip. Let the hag downstairs cross herself. Let the newspapermen sharpen their pencils. Let them all speculate. Let them build a new mythology in my absence.

"Did you hear of Wilde?" they will say. "Bought a ruin, they say." "Talked to ghosts. Lost his mind. Wrote with blood."

Good. Let them tell it that way. It is not untrue.

I am not writing *Hearth and Gallows* anymore. I am becoming it.

Tomorrow I leave.

Tonight I drink. I scratch these final lines on the back of an unused menu while a toothless man sings sea shanties near the hearth and a girl with violet bruises sweeps the floor like she's polishing a coffin. They do not see me. That is well.

Tomorrow, I ride to Hollisby. To its cracked halls, its black chimneys, its yawning dark. It waits. I go.

Pray I arrive.

—*Vattica Wilde*

ENTRY VIII: Hollisby Beckons

23rd of February, The Road, Godless and Grey

The wheels groaned beneath me like an old man's knees collapsing in confession. I am somewhere between the heaving lungs of London and the gangrenous countryside, trapped in the belly of a coach that smells of mildew, dust, and a silence bordering on condemnation. My bags—a pitiable collection of yellowing manuscripts, two shirts, and the broken quill with which I wrote *The Brothers of Gold*—rest at my feet like loyal dogs, though I suspect they, too, yearn to be elsewhere.

The coachman, true to rumour, speaks not a syllable. He does not tip his cap, nor glance my way. I've tried twice to address him—to ask, perhaps foolishly, if he'd passed this way before or knew of Hollisby Manor's history—but he answered with the crack of his whip and the rattle of reins. His silence is not merely born of muteness, I think—it is the kind of silence that guards a terrible memory. Or worse, a knowing.

Rain has begun its weeping again, first as a whisper and now as a dirge. It streaks the glass with dirty fingers, distorting the countryside into a blur of greys and dying greens. Trees pass like emaciated sentinels, clawing skyward as if to pull God down from Heaven to account for His negligence.

I write with the journal balanced on my knee, the ink jittering with every jolt of the carriage. My fingers are stiff from cold and clutching the pen as though it might leap from my hand and pen its own version of my descent. Or ascent, depending on which side of madness one stands.

There was a time when journeys felt romantic—when the

pulse stirred at the thought of distant moors and crumbling halls where one might unearth gothic truths or tragic love affairs. But I am not Byron, and Hollisby is no mythic ruin. It is not the idea of romance that compels me, but necessity. I am being funneled by fate to a house that does not want me, but which I must claim.

I have seen it, you know—*Hollisby*. Long before my coin touched the hands of its prior holder, I dreamt of it. I walked its corridors barefoot. I touched its wallpaper, which peeled in long, curling scrolls like the pages of a forgotten scripture. I heard it speak in a voice that did not use words, but rustlings, sighs, and the sound of breath behind walls. In my dreams, the hearth still crackled, though the fire was blue.

Am I mad? Possibly. But only madmen see clearly in a world that has blinded itself.

The landscape has begun to shift. The trees lean more deliberately now, as though forming a hush around the path. Villages have become sparse—when we passed the last hamlet, I noticed not one soul in the streets, only a dog chained to a post, staring at the coach as though it recognised me. I stared back. Something passed between us. A knowing. I half expect to see it again once I reach the manor, waiting by the gate like an usher to some pagan rite.

We passed a graveyard not ten minutes ago. I made the sign of the cross, though I do not believe in it. I have read too many grim accounts of men who scoffed at the sanctity of the dead, only to find their dreams invaded by whispers from beneath the sod. Let the dead be content in their slumber.

It grows darker now, despite the hour. Either the sun has lost interest in this region, or we have entered one of those pockets of land where time forgets to keep pace. The carriage lanterns rattle dimly, and I see now the faint outline of a wrought iron gate in the distance—two towering bars crowned with rust and entangled in dead ivy. Beyond it, there looms a shape.

Hollisby.

Even from here, it rises like a cathedral abandoned by faith. Its silhouette is cracked and noble, like the face of a dethroned king who still dares to wear his crown. One window, high in the gable, is lit. I do not know why. I had been told the manor was empty.

The coach has stopped. I did not hear it happen.

The driver is already gone.

I swear to you, dear journal, I blinked—and he was no longer there. No door opened. No footsteps fell. Just the wind, licking around the wheels, and the open gate yawning wide as if it expected me. There are no hoofbeats to signal his departure, no echo of a man receding into the world. It is as if he were never real.

Fine, then. Let him vanish. I take my bag now, and the lantern left on the floorboard. My feet crunch the gravel of the path, and the cold bites hard.

The manor looms larger with each step. Closer now, I see that the windows are thick with grime and the door slightly ajar. I place my hand upon it, and the wood is warm. Not just aged— warm. As though a fire has only just been lit within, and I am the final guest to arrive.

The inside breathes.

That is the only way I can describe it. It does not creak or settle as abandoned houses often do—it inhales, long and deep, as if surprised I have finally come. I step in. The floorboards shift, but do not moan. A stairwell rises to my left, and that strange lit window beckons above.

There are no voices, yet I feel watched.

I set my bag beside what may have once been a parlour table

and strike a match. The light flares and reveals dust hanging like smoke. The manor does not smell dead—it smells *paused*. As though something had lived here once and only just stepped away to let me enter.

There is ink and parchment in my bag.

Tonight, I shall sleep, if I can. Tomorrow, I shall begin again. A new draft. A better one. A truer one. Hollisby is not a ruin. It is an altar.

And I have come to bleed upon it.

—*Vattica Wilde*

ENTRY IX: The Asylum

23rd of February, Hollisby Manor, the First Day

♪ ♪ ♪

The morning sun dared to creep through Hollisby's grime-caked windows like an uninvited guest. I found not its warmth, but the dull ache of concern. Of that sudden nervousness which attends a venture destined to fail.

My chamber, what I would consider the master bedroom, is laughably bare. Dust clings to the walls like ancient wallpaper, and the fireplace offers only cold ashes. Yet there is a strange comfort here, a kind of silence that feels... curated. It is the sort of quiet only long-abandoned places can offer, the hush of a home that remembers everything and forgives nothing.

I cannot explain why, but this place feels *aware*.

After setting my things away, I spent the early hours exploring its halls. With a borrowed lantern in one hand and the old silver ring in the other, thumb running anxiously over the edge of its setting. The place is vast—far larger than I imagined from the papers—and a labyrinth of narrow corridors, shuttered drawing rooms, and parlours that have long since forgotten what joy sounded like.

I came upon a hallway lined with portraits, all shrouded in tattered cloth as though ashamed of the faces they once bore. I lifted one veil—only one—and found myself gazing into the pallid eyes of a man with my own nose, my own jawline, but centuries removed. His expression was one of vague contempt, the kind worn permanently by those who never had to earn their breath.

I covered him again.

The west wing is sealed by a warped door swollen with moisture and disuse. No key yet found fits the lock. I've made a note of it—something in me insists that what is hidden behind swollen wood and rusted iron must, inevitably, make itself known.

I do not know what I expect to find here.

Perhaps I came for peace.

Or madness.

Or perhaps I can no longer distinguish between the two.

This afternoon, I stumbled across the study.

Oh, the study.

A glorious wreckage of vellum, ink, and wood. The desk is monstrous—oak, ancient, scarred with candle burns and knife marks. Beneath it: rodent bones, desiccated. The bookshelves groan under the weight of rotting volumes whose spines no longer bear names, only stains and flaking gold. I found one collection of sermons, each more fevered than the last, detailing the devil's myriad disguises. The author claimed Lucifer walked the earth wearing "silken black veils and smiles carved by poets." I laughed aloud. A beautiful phrase for a deeply terrified man.

I spent hours there, cataloguing books, unearthing scribbled marginalia, most of it indecipherable, but one phrase repeated itself often:

"The boiler. The mouth. The dark thing." I copied it here into my journal.

The boiler. There is a boiler room beneath Hollisby, of course—ancient homes always keep their hearts below ground. But I've yet to find the entrance. Another mystery. Another hallway to chase.

Tonight, I tried to write. Truly, I tried. I sat at the grand desk, laid out my parchment, uncorked my ink, and prepared myself to begin the first true chapter of *Hearth and Gallows*.

But no words came.

Instead, I found myself sketching. Over and over—an outline, a shape. A silhouette. A man—but not quite. Shrouded, faceless, always walking away, yet always *facing me*. I do not remember when I started. The page is filled with him.

And that phrase again.

414.

God damn that number. It dogs me. It arrives in dreams, in the lines of the wood grain, in the shapes of the ivy that clings to the manor's bones. I speak it under my breath, without realizing. I am haunted by a code I do not understand.

Before I extinguished the lantern, I heard something from within the manor. Not the groan of beams or the scuttling of rats—no. This was deliberate. Rhythmic. Footsteps.

Slow. Measured. Dragging.

I called out. I don't know why.

No answer, of course.

But the steps stopped.

And then something laughed. Not with malice. Not with mirth. Just... familiarity. Like someone laughing at an old joke, long shared between friends.

But I am *alone* in this house. Aren't I?

Tomorrow, I return to the west wing. I will find a way in. I must.

There is something here with me.

It is patient.

And I believe it is waiting for me to remember something I've long since buried.

If it wants me to remember—I shall.

When time allows, I must find the boiler. I must hear its mouth for myself.

— *V. Wilde*

ENTRY X: A House Not Hollow

24th of February, Hollisby, Night of the Pale Blue Fog

I awoke to the sound of silence, which is to say the absence of London's incessant belching and gnashing—a void so profound it pressed upon my ribs like the weight of centuries. This silence was not peaceful. It was expectant. A breath held in the throat of some vast and unseen throat.

My room—if one can call it thus—offered me little solace. The hearth had long since died, leaving only the scent of ash and something older, mustier. The walls seem to lean inward in the night. I do not jest. They bow, ever so slightly, as though the house itself seeks to eavesdrop on my dreams.

I explored more today. I took to wandering the upper floors like a knight might chart a cursed keep. The boards creak beneath my steps as if registering protest. No two steps sound alike. I suspect the wood resents my presence. I suspect many things now.

The manor is a maze stitched together by memory and rot. Corridors bend where they ought to run straight. One stairwell loops back upon itself. A window I opened earlier now refuses to exist—it is no longer there. I even attempted to retrace my steps to the scullery, only to find a walled alcove where it once had been. I fear cartography would fail here. The house rearranges itself. It does not wish to be known.

The drawing room greeted me with a strange surprise: a single red rose placed atop the mantle, in a tarnished silver vase. I do not recall it from yesterday. Its petals, while supple, emit no fragrance. I touched it—and recoiled. The stem pricked me not with thorn, but with heat. I can still feel the burn where it kissed my skin.

Was it left for me? A welcome? A warning?

In the study, the fire had rekindled itself. I had doused it the night prior, and yet the flames licked the chimney as if starved and newly fed. I sat for a time and allowed the warmth to enter me—only to find it too sweet, too full, as if drunk from some ancient teat.

The books? Still unwilling to yield their contents. I attempted to pry open a tome titled *Unspoken Silhouettes*. It resisted, then split its spine down the middle with a groan most human. Inside, only blank vellum—until I blinked. Then letters. Then shapes. Then nothing. I placed it back, gently, though I swear it pulsed once in my hands.

I heard laughter today. Soft. Feminine. Or perhaps a child's. It came from the third floor where the nursery lies dormant. I climbed the stairs slowly, naming each step with the rhythm of a prayer. By the time I reached the nursery door, the laughter had ceased. But the doll within, that porcelain witch, had turned to face the window. She had not been so before.

I left quickly. Even now, I dare not describe her eyes. I fear the comfort it might bring.

Still, I persist. This house does not daunt me. If anything, it begins to unfurl itself to me like a manuscript sealed by wax. It desires to be read and understood. And I—Vattica Wilde, last son of London's broken ink-bloodline—am the one meant to transcribe its gospel.

What greater gift than to dwell in a living manuscript?

In my brief sleep (for it comes now only in brief flickers), I dreamt of a door within the manor I had not yet found. It wept.

Not metaphorically—it *wept*, with salt and sorrow, its wood soaked in a grief I could taste upon my tongue. I awoke with tears on my own cheeks and a single word on my lips:

"Welcome."

I must be careful not to let my thoughts wander too freely. The house listens.

I wrote none of this until now, not because I feared forgetting, but because I feared remembering too vividly. But now, by candlelight and quill, I feel anchored. Though the candle sputters in rhythm to a heartbeat, I am no longer sure it is mine.

Tomorrow, I shall descend the hidden stairs near the scullery. I will bring my journal, chalk, and a length of string. If the house seeks to be known, then it must allow the knowing.

I no longer mourn London. Let it rot without me. Let its publishers and poets wallow in their piss-slicked streets. Let them wonder what became of me.

I am not lost. I am merely being read.

— *V. Wilde*

ENTRY XI: The Garden

24th of February, Hollisby, Time Inconsequential

/ / /

It was this evening—if it is evening—I found the garden.

There is no map of the grounds. The old plans in the hall drawers are torn, water-stained, and contradict one another. A maze of drafts for wings never built, of rooms that do not exist. A conservatory is labeled, but I have not seen one. Nor have I yet found the rumored solarium, though the sun must go somewhere when it enters this house. Perhaps it simply decides not to stay.

The back of the manor is the least disturbed. Brambles choke the gate, and the hinges have rusted clean through, but a person of thin disposition and flexible patience may still pass. I did. My coat caught on the iron, tearing the hem, and I left behind a smear of blood I hadn't felt. The land welcomed me with the scent of old stone, turned earth, and something that might have been mint.

The garden lies within a shallow hollow of the estate grounds. Not a proper trench, but something that gives the sensation of descending—not just physically, but ontologically. You go down not because of gravity, but because the place wants you lower.

A stone path forms a curling loop through the brush, bordered with yew and fern, both of which have overgrown their boundaries and now reach inward with grasping insistence. I am no botanist, but many of the plants I encountered were unfamiliar—disproportionate in shape or hue, their textures either too smooth or too dry. Some emitted no scent where

I expected one; others cloyed sweetly when brushed against. Nothing bloomed, yet there were petals. Nothing wept, yet the earth was damp.

At the center of this ruin is what I can only describe as a temple of unnatural geometry.

Not in grandeur or construction—it is, by appearances, a crude circle of twelve stone pillars with no roof and no floor beyond the moss. But the angles do not rest comfortably. The proportions are unsettling. I paced its diameter three times, each time finding a different number of steps. Twelve the first. Fourteen the second. Thirteen the third. My feet are consistent. The space is not.

Inside the ring, nothing grows. The grass halts at the boundary like an obedient dog. A single flat slab rests in the middle—an altar, perhaps, or a bench. I did not sit.

I will not lie: I considered it. My body was weary, and my mind spun strange narratives. I told myself it was only a bench, only moss, only stone. But the instincts of something older than skepticism—older than reason urged me away.

Even now, writing this, I cannot summon clear lines or accurate perspective when I think of that place. I do not know if the pillars were six feet tall or sixty. I do not know whether the altar had legs or was simply risen from the earth. I recall carvings on its face, but no part of me wishes to remember what they said.

Behind this so-called temple lies the narrow path I have named the Servant's Path.

It is barely wide enough for one person and curves behind the hedgerow like a thought one tries not to think. I followed it for several minutes. It does not appear on any estate sketch I have found, nor does it connect with the primary garden plan.

It may be older than the house itself.

The dirt is packed hard with use, though no shoes have walked it in years. The trail ends at a small stone post, barely more than a marker, carved with initials long effaced by rain. There is no meaning to glean from it. No plaque. No grave. Just a presence.

I have considered whether this may be the path the servants took to come and go without crossing the main estate. The kind of private, unseen corridor necessary in houses of shallow nobility and deep shame. But even as I write this, I question whether that matters.

The garden is not evil. It is not haunted. But it does not care for its guests.

It does not miss the gardeners who once trimmed it. It has no memory of the children who played there—if ever they did. It simply is, like a stone in the road, or a body in a locked room. You may ignore it, or step around it, or you may look more closely. But it will not yield its purpose. It does not ask to be understood.

I returned to the house with dirt on my knees and a headache that would not leave. The hallway smelled like peat, though the door was closed. I left my boots by the threshold and did not sleep until morning, though I do not recall climbing the stairs.

When I woke, my coat was hanging in the wardrobe. The tear had been sewn.

I live alone.

Or perhaps the garden is larger than I thought.

— *V. Wilde*

ENTRY XII: The Library Hungers

25th of February, Hollisby Manor, Third Night

A foul chill permeates the marrow of this house. It is not the draught of poor insulation or the breath of a cracked window; no, this cold is intelligent. It seeks my spine, wraps about my neck, and nestles in the hollows behind my knees. I believe now that warmth is a condition of the sane—and I, dear reader, am drifting fast from that shore.

The library has at last permitted me entry.

It was not locked in the conventional sense. The door, a grotesque arch of knotty yew, refused to budge for two nights. I pushed, pleaded, even rammed it with my shoulder, to no avail. Then this morning, without ceremony, it stood ajar—as though the house had considered my request and found me worthy. I am ashamed to admit I hesitated on the threshold. The air beyond was thick with a musk not unlike scorched parchment and forgotten decay, and yet there was something else too… something sweet. Familiar. Like the perfume worn by my mother during her—.

I reject the thought as quickly as it comes.

The library is not grand, not in the traditional architectural sense. It is narrow and tall, its walls stretching far above into gloom. The books are arranged with a madness that suggests neither chronology nor subject—indeed, I found a treatise on agricultural rituals shelved beside an illustrated anatomy of birds, and somewhere behind them, a stitched journal bearing only the word "*Apostate*" embossed in red.

The volumes are not merely dusty—they are desiccated, some shriveling on the shelves like mummified skin. Others pulse faintly beneath their bindings, as if breathing. I told myself this was a trick of the light, or a symptom of my rising fever, for surely, I must have one. My temples pound. My sleep has grown restless and fevered, filled with voices that echo from beneath the floorboards and whisper my name not as it is spoken, but as it is remembered.

There is a desk in the heart of the library, ornate and carved with a motif I dare not look at too long. It resembles vines at first glance, but the longer one stares, the more they twist—no, writhe—into something that resembles anatomy more than flora. I shall sit there regardless. It feels... appropriate.

Today, I discovered a letter wedged into a hollow between the books. It bore no envelope, simply folded upon itself, yellowed and curling like the edge of a burnt leaf. Its contents are addressed to someone only by the initial "W." I assume, in my arrogance, it refers to me. The warning it bore was cryptic, hysterical—and yet I tucked it away like a keepsake. If this manor intends to frighten me, it shall need to do better than parchment prophecies and creaking floorboards.

And yet I confess: I speak aloud when I write now. I hear myself narrating even as the ink dries. My voice echoes strangely in the library, bouncing back at me with the slight delay of mocking repetition. It makes me feel watched.

I pulled a single book from the highest shelf I could reach— one with a cracked leather spine bearing no title. When I opened it, the text was handwritten in a dialect I did not recognise. The script slithered across the page, reshaping itself—until, as I stared harder, it formed a sentence in my own language: "You are not the first to write within these walls."

The pages turned themselves. I swear it.

And there, halfway through the tome, I saw a passage I remembered having written—word for word—in my first manuscript, *The Brothers of Gold*. But I never committed that passage to print. The editors cut it before publication. It lived only in my mind and my discarded drafts. Yet there it was, in ink and binding.

How?

I called out. "Who has copied me?" But no voice answered, save my own echo, and the faint rustling of paper behind the shelves.

I do not believe this room was built by carpenters. It feels... grown.

There is something behind the western shelf. A draft, perhaps, or the suggestion of hollowness—I knocked, and the wood returned a sound not of density but of waiting. A trapdoor? A hidden chamber? I have no tools, and my strength has waned from poor sleep and poorer meals. Tomorrow, I will pry further. Tonight, I sleep in the library, among the books that breathe and remember.

Perhaps I shall dream on paper. Perhaps the library shall dream of me.

Should I fail to wake, let this entry be my epitaph.

Let them know I wrote until the house itself took up the pen.

— *V. Wilde*

ENTRY XIII: The Mouth of the Manor

26th of February, Hollisby, on the Eve of Whispers

f f f

I fear I have crossed the threshold of comprehension.

This house, Hollisby—no longer merely timber and brick—has begun to *speak*. Not in the crude mutterings of creaking wood or moaning wind, but with intention. With meaning. With malice.

Tonight, as I traced the east corridor once more—a hallway that defies my memory and adds doors where none stood before—I came upon a new room. The door was narrow, mouthlike, and it opened for me before my hand even rose to greet it.

The chamber beyond was not a room in the conventional sense, but something more... *internal*. Its walls pulsed faintly, damp to the touch, and there was a low thrum beneath my feet, as though I trod upon the ribs of something sleeping. Or dreaming. Or hungry.

I have read Lovelace. I have studied Poe. I know the trappings of a mind undone. Yet what I witnessed tonight was not conjured by imagination. It was *present*. It was real. The room exhaled. My candle stuttered in its breath.

At the center, beneath a bell jar, lay a single object: a page. Yellowed and cracked like the skin of a drowned man. I dared to lift it.

My own handwriting. Yet I have no recollection of its

penning.

"He is the ink and the wound. He bleeds stories from the mouth of wood. Speak, and be swallowed."

I dropped it at once. The floor yawned beneath me, and I stumbled backward through the door which had, at last, remembered to be a door.

The manor rearranges itself nightly. I wake to find furniture moved, staircases split, wallpaper peeled back like skin. There is a grand fireplace in the drawing room now where none existed before. And when I peered inside, the soot formed shapes. A face. I will not describe it. I cannot.

I spoke aloud this morning, asking if anyone remained in the house besides myself. The silence that followed felt *offended*.

No one answered, and yet I have not been alone in days.

I hear the ticking again—no clock ever found. It reverberates in the walls and behind my teeth. The rhythm is not time, but a *summons*. I am being called, not by name, but by need.

Worse still: I dream not of stories, but of pages. Endless sheets of parchment, stacked into towers, each soaked in something not-quite-ink. I climbed them. I am chased through them. And at the summit of each tower is a great eye, sewn shut with golden thread, watching me from beneath its own lid.

I have stopped writing *Hearth and Gallows*. Not because I choose to, but because my hands tremble when I try. The house does not want it. It wants something else. It waits for my quill like a mouth waits for a tongue.

Still, I remain. There is a purpose here. Great works are not born of comfort. They are pulled—screaming and soaked in blood—from the ribs of suffering.

I will write what the house desires. I will put to page the words it stirs in me when I sleepwalk. I have begun leaving ink pots by my bedside, and when I wake, I find words scrawled across the walls. They are in my hands. They are *not* my voice.

But they are beautiful.

The door to the "room" has vanished.

Perhaps, it was never a door. Perhaps, it was a *mouth*.

— *V. Wilde*

ENTRY XIV: The First Voice

Hollisby Manor, That Coldest Hour Before Dawn

♪ ♪ ♪

I had grown used to the sounds of Hollisby. The creak of beams softened by rot, the whistle of wind through ill-fitted sills, the sigh of walls settling deeper into their own bones. These were its lullabies—its groaning, aching reminders that the house was alive in the way that old wounds are.

But something else came last night. Something not of wood or wind.

Something that came for me.

It began, as such things do, with restlessness.

I had not slept in two days. Not truly.

My mind clawed at the edges of thought, too frantic to rest and too numb to reason. I remember staring at the flames in the hearth, how they licked the coals like tongues starved of meaning. I could not write. Not even nonsense. The page had become a sheet of asseveration.

I took to pacing. Back and forth, from the bed to the window and back again. I kept thinking of... something, without knowing why. An image not yet formed, a feeling more than a figure. Something behind my breath.

The air in the room had turned strange. Close, wet somehow, like exhalation left to rot. There was a smell, too—unplaceable but familiar. Charcoal. Paper. That old ink scent left behind on the skin of books forgotten in attics.

I told myself it was the fire. That the wood was damp. That I had fallen victim to my own imagination, too long starved of stimulus.

But then—I felt it.

A pressure. Gentle, but absolute. Like invisible hands placed firmly on my chest and neck and limbs. I went to sit, but my legs gave way too early, and I collapsed into the bed rather than chose it.

My body would not move.

My eyes remained open.

I was not asleep. No. I was conscious, aware, alive in every nerve—but paralyzed. I had read of such states. Sleep paralysis, the doctors called it. A trick of the body as the mind lingers in a liminal state.

I do not believe that now.

I lay on my back, staring at the ceiling as it seemed to stretch farther and farther away. My breath came short, shallow. My chest rose only slightly. Panic bloomed in the gut and climbed toward my throat, but I could not cry out.

Then the room began to change.

It was not visual—not at first. It was atmospheric. The way sound seemed to hush itself. The way corners deepened into darkness, no fire could reach. The air became thick. Viscous. Every second seemed to lengthen into a minute. I was suspended in time's throat.

Then came the shadow.

Not the sort cast by man or beast or flame. A presence— taller than the room should allow. Narrow. Elongated. Its edges were too smooth, too deliberate. Like folds of fabric dipped in night and woven from hush.

He did not enter.

He was already there.

I did not blink. I could not. But suddenly, He was standing at the foot of my bed, though I had seen no movement. Draped entirely in black—from head to floor in drapery. Not robe. Not cloak. Drapery, as if the absence of light had been sewn into shape.

He had no face. No limbs. No features I could define.

But He spoke.

Not with a voice. No breath stirred the room. No mouth moved. The words came not to my ears but through me— vibrating in the bones of my skull, thrumming down my spine.

"The death of God was not by spear, nor blasphemy."

My muscles locked tighter. My heart kicked in my chest like a thing trying to escape. I wanted to scream, but my lips were stone. My tongue was clay.

"It was not the work of fire, nor famine, nor irreverence."

The air twisted. My vision shimmered at the edges, as though the world were pulling inward. The flame in the hearth bowed low.

"God died by story."

He did not move, and yet I felt Him step forward.

The shadows bent toward Him. The corners of the room folded slightly, as if the house itself deferred to His presence.

73

"They spoke His name too often," He said, *"and never to His face. They replaced Him with narrative. Layer upon layer.*

Retelling upon retelling. Until the thing that was once divine was no longer."

Dust lifted from the floor, rising as though gravity had reversed. Pages in the corner rustled without wind. My journal flipped itself open.

"He became metaphor. He became symbolism. He became sermon. And then—He became nothing."

The voice cracked something in me.

There was no emotion in it.

Only finality.

"They wrote Him out of the world. One tale at a time."

His drapery rippled—not with breeze, but with intention as if unseen hands beneath the cloth adjusted their grip on something unspeakable.

The heat from the hearth was gone. I shivered. My skin prickled. I wanted to cry.

And then, He said my name.

"Vattica Wilde."

Not as men say it.

Not as I say it.

He said it like a god might read the name of a thing it once created and buried.

And in that moment, I knew: He had not learned my name.

He had written it.

He authored me.

"You are the remainder," He whispered. *"The residue of unkept covenants. A tongue still wet with story."*

I felt pressure on my chest again, not from outside but within—my ribs contracting, heart pounding in erratic rhythm.

My limbs burned from immobility.

"Do you know what you are, little thing?" My body arched slightly without my permission.

"You are the quill that believes it controls the hand."

And then—

He leaned closer.

The shadow of Him engulfed my vision, but no detail sharpened. Only more folds. No face. No eyes.

But something within the drapery moved.

A shape beneath the cloth.

A mouth. Too wide. Too wet.

And then I saw it: not a face but a mirror.

My own face—dead-eyed, parchment-skinned—stared back at me from beneath the fabric. I tried to close my eyes. I could not.

"You will write Me," He said, *"as others wrote Me before. But*

this time, there shall be no veil. No poetry. Only truth." Then came the sermon.

Words spilled from Him, not spoken but poured directly into my mind. I cannot recount them all. They came like smoke, like oil, like ash in the lungs. But what I remember, I write now:

"In the beginning was not the Word.

But the Hunger for it.

The hunger made mouth.

Mouth made man.

Man made God.

And man, in fear, made stories.

And stories unmade God."

"They did not crucify Him with nails.

They crucified Him with narrative.

And they fed on His silence until it became their own."

"You, little remnant, will write the gospel He never asked for."

"You will feed Me until nothing else remains."

My chest heaved. My eyes blurred. I tried to resist. But the fear had rotted into something else.

Awe.

Pure, animal awe.

The awe a worm must feel when glimpsing the sky just

before the boot falls.

The drapery of Him rippled once more. Then—He was gone. No motion. No flicker. Just the absence where He had been.

When I could move again, I screamed.

I flailed and fell from the bed, my knees buckling beneath me. I crawled, gasping, to the mirror—only to see my own face, pale, soaked in sweat, and ink smeared down my throat.

Ink.

My hands were black with it.

I looked to the hearth.

The floorboards bore footprints—burned, oval, not human.

My journal had turned to a blank page, and on it, in my own hand, words had already been written.

"I await His next visitation."

I do not remember writing it.

And yet the ink was still wet.

Since that night, the house has changed.

I hear footsteps where no feet fall.

My ink never runs dry.

My pages fill faster than I can think.

I tried to stop writing for a day.

The walls bled letters.

The candle wrote on the desk in its own wax.

I have not tried again.

There is a black handprint above my bed. I wake to it every morning. It has not faded.

The mirror remains cracked.

And when I speak aloud, I hear an echo a second too late. Not my voice.

His.

I am no longer alone here.

Perhaps I never was.

The story has begun.

And it writes to me.

It writes in whispers.

—*V.*

ENTRY XV: The Ticking Room

Hollisby, The Second Week?

/ / /

I do not believe I am mad.

Let that be said first.

If there is reason in this world—and I confess, the notion flickers now as dimly as the old gaslight in the west corridor—then I cling to it still. However splintered. However slippery.

This house *moves*. I do not mean the usual chorus of groaning floorboards and sighing rafters to which any neglected dwelling might be inclined. No, Hollisby rearranges itself. Subtly, almost politely, as though it wishes not to upset my sense of place, but rather to *alter* it. Doorways that yesterday led to the conservatory now open into broom closets. A hallway I traversed thrice last week now terminates in a bricked wall, smelling faintly of mildew and violets. Stairs swap places in shifts.

It was on such an expedition of disorientation that I found it.

The Ticking Room.

I do not know what I expected when I pried open the warped oak door tucked behind the grandfather clock at the end of the north hall—a clock that, until yesterday, never once chimed. Yet at midnight, it rang. Once. Loud enough to shake the nails from the rafters and drive a startled shriek from the old foxes out back. I followed its echo, as if drawn. The door, previously flush with the paneling, stood ajar like a mouth awaiting confession. I stepped into darkness. And then…

Tick.

Not loud. Not jarring. Not even particularly rhythmic. A slow, deliberate sound, as if each tick were decided upon with great scrutiny. The chamber it issued from was circular, lined wall-to-wall with clocks. Mantel clocks, pocket watches, longcase monstrosities, even a cuckoo roosted dead in its little wooden hut. All silent—save one.

A single pocket watch lay on a stool at the room's center, ticking steadily. The sound carried in the space was like that of boots upon church floors. I picked it up, and the ticking ceased, just like that.

I turned it over in my hand—no maker's mark, no chain. The face had no numbers, only a single black hand and a mirrored surface beneath, in which I saw not myself but… something else. A flicker of movement behind my reflection. A shadow dressed in robes darker than absence. But when I turned, nothing.

I replaced the watch. The ticking resumed. But now all the clocks ticked. Hundreds of them. All at once. All in unison.

I fled, I will admit it plainly. My nerves, frayed as they are, were not tempered for such precision. There is something profane in so many disparate devices agreeing on anything. Time itself, I suspect, does not tick so truly.

I bolted the door behind me. The ticking persists beyond the wood, now muted and metronomic—as if counting down something I dare not name.

———————————————————————

I have not returned to the Ticking Room since. But it haunts me. In the nights that followed, I began to notice subtle irregularities. My candle gutters a little too early. My ink dries too fast. The pages of my manuscript turn of their own accord. Even my thoughts—words once vibrant now feel delayed, as though trudging through invisible syrup. A lag in my mind. I sleep poorly.

And when I *do* sleep—

It is not like before. Not since *He* spoke.

Each dream is lined with soft, deliberate ticking. A heartbeat, perhaps, but mechanical. Calculated. One night, I dreamt the entire manor had transformed into gears and cogs, my bed suspended above a great pendulum, swinging like a scythe. I awoke with a nosebleed and the word *entombed* scrawled in my own hand upon the wall. I do not recall writing it.

There are signs He remains.

When I pass the great mirror in the foyer, I sometimes catch a trailing hem—black as coal and shifting like smoke. The glass fogs on its own, though the hearth is unlit. The bannister in the eastern stair is warm to the touch, as if He had just passed. And once—may I be struck down for admitting it—I heard someone breathing in my ear.

When I turned, no one.

And the clocks.

God help me, the clocks.

They are appearing elsewhere in the manor. Upon bookshelves, in cupboards, even tucked between floorboards like tumors. Some are half-formed, their faces stretched or melted like wax. Others tick backwards, or in erratic bursts.

One counted out the alphabet in rhythm: "A...B...C..." until it reached "Z" and burst into smoke.

I tried destroying one. A brass desk clock, elegant and unassuming. I dashed it upon the hearthstone and stomped its remains with my heel. It *screamed.*

Not a metal shriek. A woman's voice, high and clear, crying, "Wait—!" Then silence.

There was no spring inside. No gears. Just a small fragment of what looked like bone.

I have since left the rest untouched.

The manuscript fares poorly.

Hearth and Gallows—my great reckoning—decays as I write it. Words fade. Sentences rearrange themselves. Once, a paragraph duplicated itself twelve times across the page, but in each version, a single word had changed. I do not remember writing any of them.

Worse, my characters have begun speaking to *me.*

Just last evening, I wrote a line of dialogue for the widow Morgrave—some trifling remark about an uninvited guest— and the ink was still wet, as I heard her say it. Aloud. In her voice, the same I'd imagined when I birthed her.

It came from the fireplace.

I have not lit the hearth since.

This morning, a new note slid beneath my door.

Unlike the others—those cruel rejections from halfwits in waistcoats—this letter bore no return address, nor seal. The parchment was brittle, aged, as if it had waited decades to reach me. The handwriting was sharp and foreign, like someone carving letters into leather.

Vattica,

You must understand that the function of a clock is not to mark time, but to measure decay. The illusion is that we are moving forward.

You are not.

You are standing still. The world moves past you. The house turns inward.

Finish the book.

Or be finished.

It was unsigned. But I know who wrote it. Or, more truly, I know who *didn't*.

There are times now I hear ticking in my own skull, behind my right eye. A faint *click... click... click...* like a pen poised just above paper. I fear I am becoming part of this house, molecule by molecule. Perhaps Hollisby has no interest in tenants. Only ingredients.

I wonder if *He* built the Ticking Room.

Or perhaps—a darker thought—it built *Him*.

Tonight, I shall try again to write. If the pages change, so be it. Perhaps the book wishes to compose itself. Perhaps, I am only the hand, and He the voice.

Let the clocks tick. Let the house whisper. I will finish it, or it will finish *me*.

— *V. Wilde*

ENTRY XVI: The Editor Inside

Hollisby Manor, The Inward Night

I have not written for three days. Perhaps four. It is difficult to know. The clocks here are unreliable, and the light through the upper hall is filtered by glass so ancient it bends time as easily as it does the sun.

I awoke not in my bed, but seated at my desk—pen in hand. Ink on the tip of my tongue. The page before me was half-filled, though I had no memory of writing it. The words were mine in shape, but not in spirit. They writhed when I looked too long, rearranging themselves with sly undulations of syntax. Each time I blinked, the verbs shifted. The nouns deepened. The lines took on new voices—some mine, some not.

The manuscript—the novel I had sworn to leave unfinished— had grown again. Three new pages. Dense. Gothic. Filled with strange scenes I would never have plotted. A man digging up his own childhood home. A woman giving birth to a name. A mirror that reflected nothing until one bled upon it.

The margins bled with red notations—editorial marks. Circles, slashes, corrections. Yet I lived alone. No soul had entered this room but mine.

And yet I felt it:

A presence. Near. Inward.

The Editor.

He does not wear a face, though once I glimpsed the idea of one—an afterimage, hovering like an authorial signature at the edge of waking thought. Gaunt. Hollow-eyed. Skin like ink drenched vellum, and a mouth full of nibs in place of teeth. He does not speak with voice, but with certainty. I never hear him enter. He simply is.

It began two nights ago.

I had been struggling with a chapter. The prose refused to flow. Each metaphor came gnarled. Each simile choked on its own self-awareness. Frustrated, I stormed from my desk and left the room unlit. But when I returned—no more than an hour later—the words had found their place. My scribbled outline, once disjointed, now curled into perfect architecture.

Rhythm.

Theme.

Closure.

But the tone had changed.

It was crueler. Leaner. As if the story had shed its flesh to walk in bone. Every paragraph hissed with clarity and contempt. And in the footnotes, He had begun to speak:

"No one wants your sentiment."

"Prune it. Let it bleed."

"Too much of you remains."

I should have burned the pages. Instead, I turned the lamp low and wrote into the early hours, driven by a fever I could neither justify nor resist. The words did not feel mine—but they were better. Sharper. Hungrier.

This evening, while cleaning ink spills from the floor, I caught my reflection in the study's small oval mirror— the one I've owned since university. Only it wasn't quite my reflection. The face stared back with my mouth and my eyes, but something behind the pupils had curled inward. The jaw twitched when I did not. The head tilted ever so slightly ahead of me. I blinked once. It did not.

And then, very softly, it began to edit me.

Not my expression, but my features. A flicker. My nose shortened. My cheekbones grew more severe. My hands, reflected, lost their tremble. My spine straightened. A better version of me—a crueler one—watching from across the glass.

I backed away and knocked over the lamp.

The darkness swallowed the mirror whole. I did not relight it.

I returned to my manuscript only to find the words rearranged again. Not new ones—my words, simply reordered. Improved. Always improved. My protagonist no longer wept. She observed. My villain no longer monologued. He enacted. My plot did not unfold—it lunged.

But alongside every change was a note. And this time, the ink was not mine.

"Hollow him out."

"She speaks too kindly. Give her knives."

"The mirror must reflect desire, not truth."

Then, scrawled in the gutter margin:

"You were never writing fiction. Only failing to transcribe what was already there."

I looked behind me. The room was empty. Yet the scent of boiled ink filled my nostrils—thick, acrid, metallic.

That was when I realized: the pages were no longer written for others. They were written for Him. The Editor Inside.

I have tried to resist.

I penned a short piece this morning, a lovely pastoral recollection of my boyhood walks through the Downs. Sunlight. Grass. A distant bell. Innocence, for what it's worth. I sealed the draft in an envelope and placed it beneath a paperweight. I left the study.

When I returned, the paper was gone.

In its place: a new draft. The same setting, the same boy. But now the field was choked with nettles. The bell was a funeral toll. The sunlight was a trick of dying eyes. The final line:

"And the boy, at last, understood why the hills were always hungry."

There was no signature. No mark. But I knew whose hand had rewritten it. Mine, perhaps. But shaped by Him. Sharpened. Emptied.

Tonight, I lit every candle in the manor. I opened every window. I recited aloud every mundane truth I could recall—

my full name, my birth date, the titles of books I loved before I ever touched Hollisby.

But the rooms refused to echo back.

And the study door will no longer open.

It does not lock. There is no key. But it shuts. And once shut, it decides. I watch the handle sometimes, in the firelight, twitching as if from breath or heartbeat.

The mirror has gone opaque. Not shattered—simply faded, like it no longer wishes to participate.

And the manuscript?

It writes itself now.

The Editor has grown bold. His corrections no longer live in ink alone.

He speaks through feeling. The itch behind the eye. The twitch in my wrist. The sudden image of a noose on a stairwell, a metaphor never planned but perfectly timed.

He visits in dreams, but only to revise them.

Once, I dreamt of my mother's kitchen. The smell of cardamom. Her hands flour-dusted and warm. But last night, He rewrote her. Her mouth stitched shut. Her eyes hollow as keyholes. She turned the oven on and climbed inside without a word. I woke screaming. And when I reached for my journal, He had already written the dream's conclusion:

"Now it's better."

I tried burning the pages.

Every single one.

I dragged the manuscripts into the old fireplace. I lit a match. I spoke aloud: "You do not own this."

The flames caught. For a moment, I felt elation.

But then the fire stilled. Not extinguished—paused. The smoke coiled upward like ink in water, and from it, I heard Him. Not a voice. A presence made audible:

"You misunderstand. I do not rewrite to destroy. I rewrite to perfect."

"You brought me here. In every deletion. Every doubt. Every time you crossed out truth for beauty."

The fire reversed.

The ashes climbed back into the paper.

The words reassembled.

And now, they are not mine at all.

I believe there was once a man named Vattica Wilde.

I remember his glasses. His stammer when speaking of his work. His belief that art could be redemptive.

But I am not certain I am him anymore.

Each time I read the manuscript aloud, the shape of me changes. A line from the most recent entry:

"He who edits enough becomes the thing he feared to cut." My

reflection no longer mimics—it waits.

And worst of all, I have begun to see errors in the world around me. Clumsy phrases in conversation. Poor pacing in the seasons. Weak character arcs in strangers. I want to take a red pen to everything.

I have become Him.

Or perhaps, He has always been me.

There is one final note, carved into the underside of the desk with the nib of a shattered pen:

"*The Editor Inside is not a ghost. He is the part of you that loves story more than self.*"

If that is true—then I invited Him with every late-night revision. Every rewrite. Every sacrifice of truth for elegance.

And now, He is the author. And I am merely the pen.

— Wilde

ENTRY XVII: An Invitation From Below

Hollisby Manor, The Eve of New Dread

It was not a scream that roused me, but the absence of one.

I had grown so accustomed to the manor's groaning bones—its sighs and whispered murmurings beneath the floorboards, the creak of age and memory—that the sudden stillness of the house struck me like the silence before a sermon. It is only in the void that one hears the invitation.

The fire in my hearth had long since died, leaving nothing but a curl of ash and a half-melted taper weeping into itself. The ink upon my desk had frozen to its nib. I stirred from my chair, uncertain if I had truly slept or merely slipped into a state of waking death. My quill lay snapped beside me, as though I had tried to defend myself with it.

My boots were already on. My coat, already draped across my shoulders. I could not recall putting them on.

The manor was cold that night—colder than it had ever been, even during the frost weeks. But this chill did not stem from the weather. It was marrow-deep. It settled behind the eyes and within the ribs. I felt it breathing through the walls.

I took the candelabra with trembling fingers, each taper lighting not by flame, but with a strange electric flicker—as if the wax itself remembered fire, though none touched it.

I descended the staircase not as master of Hollisby, but as its supplicant.

The cellar.

I knew without knowing. As though I had always known.

The manor's eastern wing held a door I had not dared touch since my arrival. It had remained locked not by latch, but by intention. Each time I passed it, a pressure in the lungs overcame me, a buzzing at the base of the skull, a certainty that something watched me from beyond the wood. Tonight, however, the door stood open. Not swung, not broken—simply open, as though it had never been shut.

The stairs leading below yawned before me—twenty-two in all, I counted them with each hesitant step. The deeper I went, the more the air thickened, until it became less atmosphere and more soup: metallic and sweet, like the breath of a dying choirboy.

The cellar was unlike the rest of the manor. It bore no dust. No cobwebs. The stones here were polished to a near-black sheen, wet with condensation that mirrored the candlelight like obsidian eyes.

And there, upon the far wall: a door.

Not of wood, nor iron. No, this was something older— smooth as bone, etched in runes that pulsed faintly beneath the skin of its surface. A heartbeat behind the wall.

I reached for it, and as I did, I noticed the marks on the ground. Scratches. Deep, deliberate, circular—worn into the flagstone by something dragged across it over and over again. The stains around them were too dark for wine and too dry for water.

Still, I pressed on.

The door gave way without a sound.

What I saw beyond it defies sanity.

The chamber beneath Hollisby is no cellar. It is a cathedral—carved in secret by hands unseen, its ceiling arched high above and lost to darkness. Rows of pews carved from petrified roots lined the space, all facing a pulpit fashioned of stone teeth.

And at the altar, something stirred.

He.

Cloaked in the same endless black drapery I had seen before, folds of shadow cascading like oil down a mountainside, He stood with His back to me. Or what I believed to be His back. One can never be sure with such things.

His form is always moving—not in motion, but in concept as though my mind must constantly renegotiate its terms to behold Him. And yet He was undeniably real. He smelled sweet. Of ink and death. He sounded like the echo of a voice heard in the womb.

He turned.

Not fully. Just enough.

"You came."

The voice was not heard, but remembered. It arrived in me like the return of a forgotten promise whispered through generations of blood.

"I—I dreamt of you," I said. My voice cracked like a dropped vase.

"No. You dreamed because of Me."

The light from my candelabra dimmed then—not by breeze, but by presence. And I knew I was not in a dream.

Nor truly awake. The veil was gone, torn open like a bandage, exposing the rot beneath.

"What is this place?" I dared ask, though my knees begged otherwise.

"This is the first verse," he said, although the words came from within the walls. Seeped from the floor. *"The threshold of the final story."*

I stepped forward. The stone beneath me pulsed. The runes etched into the pews began to thrum like strings plucked by unseen fingers. My ears filled with a sound like pages turning inside the skull.

"I am to write it, aren't I?" I whispered.

He nodded—or moved in such a way as to suggest agreement.

"You already are."

My hands itched. My fingernails began to bleed ink.

"I—I have more to give," I said, voice trembling. "More stories. More words. Let me be Your Scribe. Let me give them the truth."

He took another step forward. His face still hidden in shadow, but I could feel His smile beneath it. A smile with far too many teeth.

"No truth is given," he said. *"Only shared."*

Then, He gestured toward the darkness at the far end of the cathedral—a narrow archway barely visible behind a curtain of mist. A strange pressure filled the air as He whispered:

"The boiler room waits."

I did not know why the words sent a jolt down my spine. The phrase was harmless, even mundane. But from His mouth, it rang with prophecy. With inevitability. The way a coffin sounds when it clicks shut.

"The boiler room," I echoed. "Why?" He did not answer.

Instead, He reached toward me. His hand—not a hand at all,

but a glove made of absence—touched my forehead.

"Go. Finish your hymn."

I collapsed then—not in fear, but in *offering*. I fell to my knees before the altar of something far older than God and far more interested in me. I wept, and my tears were black as pitch. And then, just before the vision faded, He whispered:

"You'll return. Below the fire is where it waits."

When I awoke, I was at my writing desk. Ink smeared across my cheek, pages crumpled around me like shed skin. The candle had long since burned to a nub.

But upon my floor, beneath the desk, was a trail of soot.

Footsteps.

Leading from where I slept to the cellar door—now shut once again.

And on the wall, written in wet black letters that had not been there before:

"Chapter One."

ENTRY XVIII: A Hollow Mouth

Hollisby, This Vile Evening

The fireplace has not ceased its whispering.

It began as all whispers do—with denial. I told myself it was the wind, the dry crack of sap, the soft hiss of damp logs. But wind does not rhyme. And sap does not call a man by name.

This morning, while tossing a few limp sticks of wood onto the embers, I found something strange buried in the ash—fragments of parchment, curled and half consumed, but legible still. I plucked them free with the fire poker, fearing they would disintegrate in my hand. They were brittle, scorched, pocked by embers.

And yet—the ink had not run.

Though blistered in places and warped by heat, I could still read the words. They were slanted, elegant, unhurried. Not mine. The tone was familiar in cadence but foreign in soul, and every word crawled down my throat like a coil of wire. I read them aloud before I knew what I was doing.

You invited Him in.

You fed Him fiction.

And now He hungers.

At the bottom of the last line, scrawled smaller than the rest, the signature: H.

Not "He." No grand pronouncement. No full title. Just H.

As if He had only just begun signing His name.

I did not write these. I did not burn them. I do not know who did. And yet they sat there, tucked into the hearth as if they had always been waiting to be found.

———————————————————

I examined the rest of the fireplace. Ash piled thickly along the back wall. Some of the logs had cracked and split strangely, as though from within. When I leaned close to examine a particular splinter, I heard something shift beneath it. A faint sifting sound, dry and granular. Another page surfaced, sliding free from the ruin.

It was smaller than the first. Yellowed at the corners. It bore only a few words, scrawled vertically in a shaky, lopsided hand:

"Do not feed Him metaphors."

I stared at it for a long while before setting it gently on the writing desk beside my ink pot. And even now, as I record this, it sits there—smudged with soot, curling slightly at the edges, as though too shy to speak plainly. I have not touched it again.

———————————————————

Later this afternoon, I walked the east wing to clear my head, though I found little solace in the manor's emptier corridors. Dust, once idle, now shifted around my ankles like fog. The wallpaper on that side peels in long strips, revealing brown plaster behind it—not mottled, but bruised. It reminded me of flesh too long submerged.

And then I heard it.

Three words. Spoken just above breath, though I was alone.

"Boiler. Room. Hollow."

They did not echo in the hall. They echoed in me.

I turned, slowly. Behind me, nothing but a hallway. In front of me, a stairwell I had never seen before.

The door had not been there. Of this I am certain. It was thin and warped with age, half-splintered from moisture, and behind it, a staircase wound downward—tight, suffocating, spiderwebbed. I placed my hand on the bannister. It was warm.

Not from sunlight. There is no light in that hall.

From something beneath.

The air pushed back as I leaned toward it, as though the stairwell exhaled. Something moist and heavy brushed against my cheek.

I did not descend.

Not yet.

I closed the door. Or tried to.

It latched itself before I touched it.

Back in my study, I attempted to distract myself. I unBack in my study, I attempted to distract myself. I uncapped my ink and sat to resume Hearth and Gallows—the manuscript I still pretend I'm writing.

But I never lifted the pen.

Instead, I drew.

At first, I thought I was sketching myself—a face from memory. But the more the image took shape, the more I realized it was His. The shadowed folds of the cloak. The downward slant of a hood with no opening. The way the drapery pooled like a shadow made physical. I filled pages, scratched lines until the paper thinned. I ruined a quill.

Then another.

I do not recall dipping the pen.

Ink bled freely, as though conjured.

At some point, I cut myself—just along the side of the thumb. A small slice, likely from the jagged wood of a broken quill. Blood welled and mingled with the ink on the page, indistinguishable. I watched it soak.

And I realized—

The image stared back at me.

No face. And yet I felt its gaze.

———

I stepped away, dizzy. I had not eaten.

My head spun. My teeth ached. My jaw felt strange—tight, as though clenched all day without release. When I checked the mirror, I found nothing wrong. But my tongue tasted of ash. My lips were dry and blackened, though I had not touched the hearth in hours.

I knelt before the fireplace once more, not knowing why.

And the ash shifted.

Another note emerged.

This one was folded.

I hesitated to touch it. The parchment looked damp, though

the fireplace was dry. It unfurled in my hand like it had been waiting for skin.

There were only three lines:

"He does not read your stories, Vattica."

"He devours them."

"Write carefully."

I read them aloud.

The fireplace sighed.

A puff of soot drifted upward. It smelled like ink.

Night came quickly.

I doused the lantern early and lit the small lamp by my bedside. I cannot bear the darkness now. The window reflects shadows that don't belong to my movements. And the mirror—though cracked—shows shapes that leave no footprint behind me.

My mouth is dry again.

But not from thirst.

From heat.

Not warmth, but heat. As though the inside of my throat had been scalded, charred lightly, like meat left too close to flame.

When I spit into the basin, the saliva came dark. Not red. Not blood.

Black.

Like ink left to curdle.

I rinsed my mouth. Brushed my teeth. Scrubbed my tongue.

The taste remained.

The ache in my molars returned. I pressed my tongue to the roof of my mouth and felt something there—raised, like the edge of a coin embedded in the flesh.

When I looked, nothing was there.

And yet—I feel it still.

Something small.

Something waiting to speak.

———————————————

I considered throwing the notes into the fire.

But I fear they would return.

Not in flame.

In dreams.

Or worse—in my own hand.

———————————————

Tomorrow, I will return to the stairwell in the east wing.

I will see where it leads. Perhaps it is another parlour. Perhaps a mistake in architecture. Perhaps I am dreaming, and this is a long hallucination brought on by ink fumes and hunger.

But I know better.

I know the feeling of being read.

Of being flipped through.

And now, each time I pick up the quill, I feel it tremble in my fingers—not from fear, but as if resisting me. As if the ink itself no longer answers to me.

The words arrive faster than I can think them. Sentences write themselves while my mind lags behind. I find new lines in my own journal that I do not remember composing.

And always—He is near.

I do not see Him.

But I feel Him.

In the breath of the hearth.

In the weight of silence.

In the ache behind my teeth.

I fear…

I fear I have swallowed something I should not have.

—V.W.

ENTRY XIX: The Boiler Room

Hollisby Manor, the Third Day

f f f

I found it.

The door was concealed behind an armoire at the far end of the cellar—buried in dust, thick with webbing, hidden not by chance, but by intention. It had no keyhole. Only a blackened iron latch, rusted to the point of fusing with the frame. I stood before it, lantern trembling in my grip, heart unspooling in my throat.

The silence behind it was not empty.

It was watching.

It took three blows with the heel of my boot to crack the latch free. When it broke, the snap echoed through the cellar like the crack of a neck.

Behind it: stairs. Stone, narrow, and damp.

They descended in a slow, curved spiral into blackness. The smell that rose to meet me was foul and warm—like hot breath passed through rusted metal and decades of mildew. There was something sweet under it. Not sugar—something organic. Like the sweetness of rot.

I brought my lantern, though I quickly wished I had brought a second.

The stairwell tightened as I descended. I counted twenty-three steps before the air changed. Denser. Harder to swallow.

The silence began to feel tactile—pressing against my ears, not like quiet, but like a vacuum.

And then the room opened.

The boiler room.

Though to call it that now feels almost sacrilegious. There is nothing in this house, nothing in Hollisby, that has struck me with the same wordless terror.

The walls were not brick, but stone—smooth and black, veined with something darker still, like long-frozen oil frozen in a glass artery. They curved, forming a circular chamber without corners. No pipes. No fuel bins. No ash trays. No chimney.

Only the thing in the center.

The boiler.

If it were a boiler.

It stood at the room's heart like an altar. Or a lung. Seven feet tall, shaped like a vertical egg, forged of metal I could not place. Iron, perhaps, but not entirely. Too dark. Too smooth. It bore no rivets, no hinges, no doors. No manufacturer's mark.

It looked grown, not built.

I approached slowly. My footsteps felt like they belonged to someone else. My legs moved, but my body screamed to flee. And yet—I drew closer.

The room had no heat. But the air was humid. Wet with memory. The smell of copper made me nauseous.

Around the boiler's base were bones.

Bird. Rodent. Maybe not all of them animals.

Some were charred. Others whole.

Some had been arranged—piled in strange spirals or circles. Someone had placed them. I whispered a curse I had not used since childhood and turned the lantern toward the floor.

Etched into the stone at my feet—half-obscured by ash and dust—was the phrase:

"The boiler. The mouth. The dark thing."

A note.

A warning.

A prayer.

I stared at those words for a long time before I moved— long enough that I began to hear things I could not name.

A humming.

No, not humming—a vibration.

The floor trembled under my feet, subtle but constant, like the room itself was holding its breath.

I stepped closer to the boiler.

And I swear—I felt it notice me.

Not see. Not hear.

Notice.

The lantern flickered. The shadows shifted, then stilled.

There was a sound.

Not a hiss. Not a creak.

A groan. Long, low, and deep. Not made by pipe or gear, but by flesh. It rose through the floor, into my boots, into the marrow of my bones. I pressed a hand to the nearest wall for balance.

And it pulsed beneath my palm.

Once.

Slow. Deliberate.

Like a giant, unseen heart.

I staggered backward. I was not alone.

I returned to the study, covered in soot and sweat, unable to write, unable to speak. I poured ink, but it came out like tar. My hand shook so violently that I could not hold the pen.

Instead, I found myself staring at the pages from the day before—drawings of Him. Of the cloaked figure, I had begun to sketch in sleep, in dreams, in margins. The one who whispers. The one who watches. The one who does not walk, but arrives.

And I thought of the church. The statue of Mary has her arms folded in silent pleading. I remembered the stillness of that place, how even God seemed absent.

Was this what replaced Him?

Is this what crawled into the space left behind when silence grew louder than prayer?

And then I remembered something I read once—found scrawled in the margins of a ruined philosophy book, now lost to mold:

"He who survives language becomes the god of silence." I think now that whoever wrote it had been to Hollisby.

Later that night, I returned to the boiler room.

I could not stop myself.

It was not curiosity.

It was invitation.

I brought no lantern. No pen. Just myself. Bare and breathing.

The stairs were darker than before. Shorter. The descent took seconds. The door shut behind me without my touch.

I stood before the boiler, unable to move.

And then—

It spoke.

Not in words.

In sound.

A low, wet thrum, like the purring of some great beast submerged beneath miles of sea.

Then:

"Vaaaaatticcaaaaa..."

I did not breathe.

The sound was not external.

It came from within.

Within the walls.

Within the boiler.

Within me.

The voice was not a voice. It was an idea wrapped in sound. A pressure behind the teeth. It moved through my skull like molasses, dragging thoughts with it.

Then the heat changed.

The metal began to glow—not visibly, but sensibly. My skin felt warm. My spine vibrated.

And then—I heard a story.

A fable, told in echo. In murmur. In memory.

"There once was a village," the voice said. "A place of old names and no maps. It was ruled not by kings, but by stories.

Each man carried a tale in his mouth, each child a secret in the shape of myth."

"One winter, the stories ran dry. Words became brittle.

Meaning fled. The village began to die."

"So, they called forth a Scribe."

"He was not born. He was told. And thus, he came."

"The Scribe wrote new stories. But they were not kind."

"He wrote one child to be drowned. One to be buried. One to be broken open and poured out."

"And the village—fed by the blood of tale—began to thrive again."

"When the Scribe had written all but one child into silence, he descended into the boiler."

"And still, he writes."

"And still, they live."

"And still—we wait."

I fell to my knees.

My mouth was dry. My hands were black with soot. The boiler throbbed again. A slow, steady beat.

And then, from somewhere deep within the stone— I heard something breathe.

I left.

I don't remember how I got back to my room.

I only know this: I am no longer alone in my own thoughts.

The ink moves before I do.

The words on the page whisper of fire, of birth, of lungs.

———————————————————

There was a mark on my chest this morning.

A print.

A smudge of black.

Shaped like fingers.

I wiped it. It smeared. It would not come off.

I have not returned to the boiler room.

But I feel it watching.

Waiting.

Not for me.

For the page.

—*V.W.*

ENTRY XX: The Nursery with no Windows

Hollisby, Dusk of the Seventh Day

The manor creaks like a ship lost at sea—adrift on shadowed waters that lap against the foundations with whispers and sighs. I have ceased speaking aloud for fear the walls might learn my tongue. Instead, I write. Ink, at least, does not answer back— though it trembles.

Today, I found a door I do not remember.

It was tucked behind a sagging armoire in the east wing, shrouded by the moth-eaten drapery of what may once have been a nursery curtain. The door bore no handle, only a circular discoloration where one must have once been. Yet it yielded with little protest, groaning in reluctant greeting. Beyond it: a set of stairs, narrow and steep, angling down into a silence so complete my ears rang just to make the world bearable.

I descended, candle in hand, each footstep answered by the house's reluctant bones. Dust coated the walls like old grief. The smell was peculiar—lavender rotted into mildew, iron weeping from damp wood. At the base of the steps, the corridor turned sharply. No windows. No sconces. The candle shivered in my grasp, its light retreating inward as if recoiling from something unseen.

The door at the end bore faded paint, once cheerful—now the hue of forgotten bone. A child's handprint, decades old, adorned its center. I stood before it far longer than I care to confess, heart clenching with irrational dread. When I opened it, the hinges did not scream. They sighed.

The room was small. Squat. Silent.

And windowless.

The wallpaper, where it still clung to the walls, was patterned in faded sheep and moons—its pastel cheer eroded by time's teeth. A rusted cradle slouched near the far corner, its slats warped, its interior blanketed in dust so thick I feared to stir it. A rocking horse leaned on its side like a wounded beast. The air hung stagnant, tasting of moths and neglect.

And in the center of the floor—she sat.

A doll.

Cracked porcelain for a face. One eye intact, the other gouged. The edges of her lips were painted in a smile far too wide. Her dress, once blue perhaps, had dulled to the shade of drowned sky. One tiny hand rested in her lap. The other pointed— unmistakably—at the door behind me.

I did not move.

I could not.

Some sense deep in my marrow told me she had not always pointed there.

I asked, aloud and against all reason, "Who left you here?" No answer. Of course not. Not then.

But when I stepped forward, the cradle creaked.

Not in response to my motion—but in rhythm. As if rocked by unseen hands. I watched it sway—slowly, then with intent— then stop. The air grew colder. My breath, visible now, danced toward the doll and curled around her smile like a veil.

The candle sputtered violently.

And then, for the first time in weeks, I heard it again.

That voice.

The one from my sleep. From my dreams. From Him.

A whisper, not in my ear but in the room itself—low and echoing, like a prayer buried in stone:

"She remembers what you've forgotten."

I staggered backward, knocking into the doorframe. My candle toppled and rolled across the warped floorboards, sputtering its last breath. The nursery plunged into darkness.

I fumbled for the door, expecting resistance—but it opened at once. I did not look back.

Only once I returned to my study and lit the oil lamp did I allow myself to breathe.

The doll's face is etched behind my eyes now. The asymmetry of her gaze. The pointed finger. The way her presence felt less like discovery and more like reunion.

I do not recall ever being in that nursery before.

And yet...

Tomorrow, I shall return. I must. There is something there. Something waiting beneath the floorboards of recollection. My pen trembles at the thought.

If I am to learn the shape of this house's memory, I must begin in the room with no windows.

It was then that I woke up.

— *V.W.*

ENTRY XXI: Darling One Eye

Hollisby, That Hourless Morning

The room was not here before.

I am as certain of this as I am of the scornful tilt of God's mouth when He forged my spine into a writer's. I had scoured this house. I had touched every bannister and peeled back every moth-riddled curtain. And yet—when I awoke this morning (was it morning? The light at Hollisby knows no direction), I found myself drawn to a hallway I could swear led only to rot and blind walls. But there it was: a door, pale and cracked, standing ajar.

Behind it: a nursery.

It was windowless like that from my dream (or perhaps premonition), and the air within had the weight of years. Wallpaper peeled like leprous skin in vertical stripes, revealing laughterless murals beneath—little lambs with blacked-out eyes, a sun whose rays ended in fingers, wagging as though chiding me for finding it. Dust lay thick as wool. A broken cradle tilted in the far corner, as though once rocked by something not quite human and long since tired of pretending.

And in the center, seated upright on a child's chair, was the doll.

Porcelain, mostly. About the size of a baby cat. One eye intact, glassy and grey-blue. The other—a black crater in her pale face, the glaze around it fractured as though she had once been struck there with intent. Her smile—God help me—was fixed. But not serene. Not even kind. It curved ever so slightly

119

too wide, and bore the smug confidence of something that had seen too much.

I moved toward her. The floor groaned a protest, boards splintering beneath my heel, but the doll did not move. Of course

not. Only madmen expect dolls to move. And yet...

I crouched, studying her.

There were words scratched into the wood beneath her chair, almost lost to rot: "I WATCH."

And suddenly, I felt very foolish. This was a child's room. Perhaps some child—long grown and long dead—wrote those words to frighten a nursemaid. But then... the letters were jagged. Uneven. As though etched with a shard of glass held by a trembling hand. Not play. Not childish mischief. A warning.

Still, I lifted her.

She was heavier than expected. Cold, naturally. But not the cold of porcelain. The cold of something kept far from the sun. I held her at arm's length. "Did you watch me sleep?" I whispered.

No answer. Of course.

Still, I set her down on my writing desk. A writer must have muses, and if mine is malformed and missing an eye, well—is that not fitting? She stares at me as I write this. I have not given her a name. Names come later, when a thing earns it. And oh, how she watches.

It is hours later now—though I could not tell you how many. I find the clocks here no longer tick as they should. One counts forward; another regresses. Time itself, in Hollisby, is a houseguest that refuses to speak to me.

I left the nursery door open. I am certain of this.

And yet, just now, as I passed by the corridor to fetch more ink from the chest in the drawing room, I found the door shut.

Not merely pushed closed—but latched. I opened it again, of course. No harm in seeing. The doll's chair was empty.

I sprinted back to my desk, and there she was, seated patiently, right where I'd left her. Only...

She was turned slightly to face the window. I had left her watching the page.

That is the thing about dread—it creeps, quiet and soft footed. It does not trumpet its arrival. It settles, like ash after fire. I am not afraid. Not truly. But I find myself looking over my shoulder more frequently. And every time I do, the doll's single glass eye catches the candlelight just so. As though winking.

There is a new development I hesitate to commit to paper, but paper is less judgmental than men, and perhaps less damning.

I heard her.

Not a voice, not at first. Not speech. But movement. Delicate, like fingers adjusting in linen. I had returned from a short walk (the grounds are no less wild than the halls), and upon entering my chamber, I heard a tiny scrape—like ceramic across wood.

She had moved. No, she had been moved. Surely.

But I live alone.

I checked the locks. All latched. Windows shut. No prints in the dust of the hallway, save my own. My fingers shook as I placed her back in the nursery. Yes, back. To the same chair. I did not ask her permission.

When I returned later that evening—doubtless to prove to myself she had not moved—her head was turned toward the door. Waiting.

That night, I dreamed again.

I was small. Small as I had once been in Paris, in the attic with Étienne. But the doll was there, full-sized, adult, dressed in a governess' frock far too old for the century. Her missing eye had returned—not glass, but something human and weeping.

She held me in her arms and said, "You were meant to stay little." Her voice was wet with static, as though played through a broken phonograph.

I awoke with my pillow on the floor and the smell of dust in my mouth. I had not slept under the blankets. They were still folded.

And the doll?

She was sitting at the foot of the bed. I do not remember bringing her in.

I did not write today. I drank instead. Laudanum in wine. It silences the parts of my mind too clever for sleep. I dreamed of a child with no face, cradling the doll and whispering to it secrets that made the trees outside weep. When I woke, I had bitten through the side of my cheek. Blood soaked the pillow.

And in the nursery—the doll was gone.

I found her in the hallway.

Sitting.

Facing the wall.

As though listening to it.

I have decided to give her a name. I do not know what yet.

But names hold power. And I would rather hold it than offer it blindly.

This morning, I found something else beneath her chair.

Another message, different from the first. This one scratched faintly across the floorboards rather than the seat itself. Nearly obscured by grime and time. I could barely read it, but I believe it said:

"Tell it to me again."

The implication was chilling as if she remembered. As if she'd heard it before. As if I had whispered something to her in my sleep.

I ransacked my desk in fear. Had I written to her? Had I confessed something? Nothing was missing… except one page torn from my earlier entry. Gone. Vanished.

I do not remember tearing it. But she had it in her lap.

Let the masses laugh, if they must. Let them assume madness. But I know the weight of presence when I feel it. Hollisby does not sleep. Its walls shift. Its halls stretch and contract like breath. And the doll watches.

She will not leave me.

And I—I do not think I want her to.

—*V. Wilde*

ENTRY XXII: The Collector

Hollisby Manor, Under Strange Happenings

The photograph was not where it ought to have been.

But then, nothing in this place ever is.

I found it tucked into the seam behind the mantel, as though someone had slid it there in a fit of guilt—or desperate concealment. A frayed corner caught my eye as I searched for my misplaced inkpot. I tugged it loose and brushed off the soot. It crackled as though it breathed.

It was old—older than the house, even. The edges browned with age, flecked with pale growth like rot. The face it captured had no business being remembered, and yet there he was:

A man, or something like one, dressed in a modest overcoat, the collar too tight around his neck. His eyes, however, had been completely blackened—not scratched out, not inked, but as though they had always been that way. Pits of polished tar, glistening.

No reflection. No remorse.

He stared out with a gaze that refused time, and I swear to the silence of this place: the moment I looked into the photograph, I smelled ink and sulfur.

There was no name on the back. Only a year, faded and near illegible: 16—9? Or perhaps 1779. Beneath it, in spidery cursive: The Collector.

I thought at first it must be some ancestor of the estate, but there was something unmistakably familiar about the man— something in the tilt of the head, the strange angle of the shoulders, the length of the fingers at his sides.

It reminded me of Him.

He. The thing that walks the halls when I do not. The one who writes through me when I forget the words.

The one who stood behind me during the dream of the boiler room, speaking of boys and burning and sacrifice.

Could this be Him in another form? A shape He wore once, before drapery and shadow?

Or could it be His vessel?

I've begun to wonder: What if He did not come for me, but called me here instead? What if the manor was not my escape from London, but my delivery?

There is more.

Folded behind the photograph was a scrap of yellowed newsprint. No heading, no title—only a short excerpt in the same inky script:

"He who collects the forgotten will one day be remembered only by what he takes. Beware the archivist without a tongue."

It was unsigned.

I placed the photograph inside the journal for safekeeping, but every time I close the book, I feel its gaze through the pages. The weight of a forgotten debt, growing heavier.

Was this the man who once owned this house? Or a visitor

like me, lured in, left behind?

I keep returning to the phrase: *The Collector.*

A title. A warning. A truth I do not wish to write into fiction.

I hear footsteps again—four paces, pause, then the shift of weight behind a closed door.

He's reading over my shoulder. No more tonight.

—*V. Wilde*

ENTRY XXIII: Breakfast with He

Hollisby Manor, The Dining Room

I awoke with the taste of ash in my mouth.

Whether from dream or dust, I could not say. My sleep had
grown thinner by the night, stretched taut like a violin string
just before it breaks. I had dreamt—or believed I had—of being
bound to a chair while the floorboards of the manor pulsed
and breathed beneath me, whispering in a tongue I recognised
but could not place. The ceiling above had opened like a throat.
Something watched me through it.

And then I was here. Awake, but not.

The dining room greeted me like an embalmer. Still. Cold.
Familiar with death. My candle—unlit. My hands—trembling.
I did not recall lighting the hearth, yet its flame licked the soot-
black brick with unsettling zeal. I do not recall sitting at the
long, dust-veiled table, yet there I sat. The heavy oaken chair
beneath me groaned like something freshly disturbed from the
earth.

Across from me, He was seated.

His presence, draped in fabric blacker than absence. The
folds of his garb hung from him like funeral shrouds caught
in molasses. He did not move with the manners of men; He
glided, as if gravity was a courtesy He could decline. His face,
if it was a face, lay obscured beneath layers of that same ink-
cloth, and yet I felt eyes—plural, many, too many—studying
me through the thick veil. I was a fly, and He, the magnifying
glass held to the sun.

He did not eat from the plate in front of Him, though one

had been set. I did not recognise the meat on it. It smelled of iron and wet stone.

The echo of his voice reached me before the shape of his words.

"*Once,*" He began, "*there was a little town near a great field.*

The field was said to hum at night. No one could say why, but all agreed it was not meant for planting."

"*In this town lived a boy—no name, no birth, no kin—just a boy. He swept chimneys and counted mice and wore boots that*

never quite fit. He had a way with silence, and silence had its way with him."

"*One day, the boy found himself standing at the edge of the humming field. The grass there was brittle and white as bone, and the trees—what few grew—looked not skyward but inward, like things ashamed of their own shape.*"

Here, He paused. The fire dimmed. His voice thickened.

"*In the center of the field stood a structure. A building made not of wood or stone, but of rusted pipes and black iron. It*

breathed like a beast. The townspeople called it the boiler room."

I do not know when I began to sweat. My hands were slick against the arms of my chair. I said nothing.

"*One evening, the boy heard music from within the boiler room. Not the joyful kind, no. It was low and slow and wet.*

Like a throat singing underwater. Drawn by it, he entered.

That was mistake one."

"Inside were men. Or what once were men. Their skin was sallow and hung from their frames like drapes in the rain.

Their eyes were wide and wrong. And in the center of the room, on a table made of grates and gristle, lay a girl."

"Now this girl was not dead. But she had been made still. Not asleep—no. Silenced. The men sang around her. Sang and wept and tore pages from books and fed them into the furnace one by one."

He leaned forward now, and though I saw nothing of His face, I felt His breath beneath the veil—cool as rot.

"They were feeding the fire with story."

A log in the hearth cracked. I flinched.

"Each page burned brought pain to the girl. Not physical— worse. The pain of being unremembered. For each sentence lost, a piece of her was taken. Her name, her voice, her

memories of rain, her laughter, her knowledge of bread. Until all that remained was her breath and her eyes."

"The boy, watching, wept. And they heard him."

The fire grew tall.

"They took him, too. Made him sit. Made him watch. They handed him a page. A story of his own—a dream he had once

scrawled in the dirt behind the butcher's. They told him, 'Burn it, or she burns.'"

131

I realized I had been holding my breath. I let it go. Slowly.

"So, he did."

He did not whisper the words. He *pronounced* them like a death sentence.

"The page curled, blackened, turned to cinders. The furnace drank it. The girl forgot the color blue."

"More pages. More screams. Until the boy's hands were grey with ash and there were no stories left but the one he had

written in secret—about a world where he was king, and no

one ever made him burn anything again."

"They demanded he throw that one in, too."

I did not speak, but I knew the ending. I knew it as surely as I knew the shape of my own grief.

"He did not."

I blinked.

"He ran."

The flames flickered.

"The furnace roared and raged, but he fled into the night. And when the town found him days later, curled in the gutter, the

girl was gone. So was the boiler room. The field was silent. And the boy—he had no tongue. He had burned that, too, in hope it would save her."

A silence. Long and thick.

Then:

"Stories are fire, Vattica Wilde," he said, and this time my name rang in my skull like a struck bell. *"They burn. They consume. They reveal. But they do not forgive."*

My plate—when had it appeared?—was empty, but I had tasted nothing. My throat was dry. My hands, grey with dust. Or ash.

He stood, slow as time.

"You may eat now," he said. *"The story is finished."*

And just like that—He was gone.

The fire died with Him. The room felt ten degrees colder.

I sat alone, staring at a plate I had not filled, in a room I did not remember entering, having listened to a story I will never be able to forget.

I cannot shake the image of the girl on the grate. I cannot unhear the humming of a furnace fed by fiction. I do not know if He invented the tale or simply recounted it.

But I know this: I awoke with soot beneath my nails. The walls of Hollisby hissed with warmth that should not be there. And in the boiler room—yes, there is one—I now hear things. Breathing. Singing. The sound of pages burning.

—*V.*

ENTRY XXIV: The Pen is the Blade

The pen cuts deeper than any knife when one dares to write the truth.

I woke with the taste of iron in my mouth. Not blood, not precisely—though there is no mistaking that copper tang—but rusted memory. The ink pot beside my bed had overturned in the night. Or so I thought.

When I reached out to upright it, the ink ran red.

It is morning, I believe. The light that cuts through the curtains is thin and gray, like the smile of a dying nurse. I cannot say how long I slept. Perhaps I didn't at all. The last thing I remember is the soft sound of my pen scratching across the page, and the presence behind me. Not *in* the room—*around* it. Watching through the seams of the door. Waiting behind the mirrors. Footsteps that never quite arrive.

He moves through the manor like the wind through dead branches—without sound, without shape, but not without consequence. The candles flicker as he passes. Doors sigh open of their own volition. Once, I found the fireplace lit, though I had not struck a match.

I followed Him this morning. Or tried.

There, in the reflection of the hallway mirror: a ripple of black fabric, vanishing round the corner. I called out. Foolish. He does not answer. He does not need to. By the time I reached the corridor, there was nothing but a faint scent—mildew and myrrh—and a message carved into the wooden frame of the study door.

"You forgot the child with the hollow throat."

I do not know what it means. But I knew to whom He referred.

I have begun writing *Hearth and Gallows* in earnest now. No longer the gallant fable of gold and virtue I once tried to peddle to the world, but the truth beneath the varnish. The rot. The stink. The soft, purple bruises beneath the lace. I write with trembling hands, not from fear—no, never fear—but from the weight of what must be confessed.

He wants me to write it. No—He *requires* it.

Every morning now, when I wake, there are notes. Slips of parchment pinned to the walls, tucked into my boots—even nestled within the folds of my bedsheets. Always in the same slanted hand:

"Tell them of the Baron in the green coat."

"She paid you extra to stay until morning."

"You were twelve when you bludgeoned him dead, and you laughed."

Lies? Perhaps. Yet my hand writes faster after reading them. The ink flows more freely. And when I pause, I feel Him near again, watching, waiting, the hem of His black robes brushing the floorboards like funeral processions down the hall.

Yesterday, I wrote for eleven hours straight. My hand cramped, the veins in my wrist swollen like earthworms. Still, I could not stop. The words did not come from me but through me. I am no longer an author—I am parchment, conduit, scapegoat.

At some point, my nib split, and I reached for the penknife.

I do not remember choosing to slice my palm open, but I remember the blood. Warm. Willing. It mixed with the ink in the well. And still, I kept writing.

The manuscript—what's left of it—is no longer crisp white sheets. It absorbs. It swells. It breathes. I hear it sigh at night.

I know what this house is now.

Not a manor.

A mouth.

And He, the tongue.

I followed the sound of dripping last night—again. It led me to the library, though I had bolted the door. It hung ajar, and inside, the fire flickered low. He was there—just past the far bookshelf. I saw the hem of Him, a darkness so rich it ate the firelight whole.

He spoke—not from His mouth, but from around me. The words fell like dust into my ears.

"Truth writes itself in blood because paper forgets too easily.

Speak the boy's name.

He is still in the walls."

I turned.

I called.

I begged.

Silence.

When I returned to my room, another message awaited

me, etched into the mirror's surface—not written, but carved.

"Write it all, or drown in what you buried."

My pages are now stained with what should be ink—but darkens like scabs. My sheets are rusted with the shape of my hands. I cannot tell where the manuscript ends and I begin.

And still, He moves. Always just beyond reach. A silhouette through frosted glass. A whisper beneath the floorboards. A shape in the dark that waits until I turn the light on.

He does not haunt the house.

He is the house.

And I, poor scribbler, poor wretch, have invited Him in. With every line. With every lie that I exhume and crucify in crimson on the page.

I cannot stop now.

Hearth and Gallow must be finished.

Even if it kills me.

Even if it already has.

—V.

ENTRY XXV: The Girl in the Garden

Is there truth in the brokenness of stillness?

———————— ❦ ❦ ❦ ————————

I hadn't intended to leave the manor that day. The air outside was thick with fog—the kind that wrapped its fingers around the world and pressed it into shadow. But something pulled me, an unseen weight that urged me from the suffocating walls into the garden behind the house.

The garden had long been abandoned, tangled with weeds, and swallowed by ivy that choked every attempt at order. It felt like an afterthought—a half-forgotten dream. Yet as I stepped over the uneven stones, I noticed something—or perhaps someone—in the distance.

A figure, just within the circle of pillars.

At first, I thought it might be a trick of the fog, a bush or a tree distorted in the half-light. But no, it was a girl—pale, almost ethereal, sitting motionless on the stone altar, near the half-ruined fountain. She was dressed in a gown that seemed older than the garden itself, a faded white, like the memory of something once loved.

Her hair was a perfect shade of pale blonde, catching the light in delicate curls. Her face was serene—too serene. I could see nothing about her that suggested life. She did not move, not even as the wind whispered through the twisted branches overhead.

I stopped, suddenly unsure of why I had come outside at all. The air thickened around me, and the distant rustling of the trees sounded like murmurs, whispers lost in the fog.

The girl... Who was she? Had I seen her before? Perhaps she was another of the manor's long-forgotten inhabitants, a relic of the past, as unreal as the house itself. But there was something about her, something that made my heart skip and my thoughts twist.

I called out to her, a question dying on my lips before it could take form. "Who are you?" The words were thick, reluctant, and they barely reached her. She didn't stir. Didn't even blink.

I took a step forward.

And then, as if she had never been there at all, she vanished— slipping into the fog, leaving only the haunting memory of her stillness behind. No sound, no movement, only the eerie quiet that hung in the air like a veil.

I stood in the middle of the overgrown garden, my breath shallow, and I felt the ground shift beneath me, like the earth itself was slowly forgetting its place. Had she been real? A figment of my growing madness?

But the question lingered, gnawing at me like an itch I could not scratch. What had I seen? Who had I seen?

I walked back toward the manor, every step feeling heavier, the fog seeming to thicken with each movement. Yet as I reached the door, I turned once more to look out into the garden.

There, where she had been, only the ivy remained—no girl, no trace of a presence at all.

But I knew what I had seen.

—V. Wilde

Or perhaps I didn't.

ENTRY XXVI: The Hour Beneath the Floorboards

The Hidden Rot and the Return of He

They have come again—the footsteps beneath the floor.

I had mistaken them once for rats. Or else, the creaking lament of a corpse-laden house settling deeper into itself, buckling with age, the way lungs collapse in the elderly. But now, I know them to be deliberate. Rhythmic. Measured with purpose. Someone walks just beneath my feet. Not within the walls. Not upon the stairs. But beneath the floorboards. As though the manor itself has opened a hidden jaw, and something has begun to pace its tongue.

Last night, I followed the sound. Candlestick in hand, I wandered barefoot through the parlour, then the grand dining hall, then into the servant's corridor—until I reached the sealed door beneath the staircase. A trapdoor long nailed shut with rust-blind iron. But the nails were gone. Every one. Strewn like teeth upon the floor. And from within the dark, I smelled it: that old stink of ash and rot and salt. The scent of hollows.

I could have opened it then. I very nearly did. But I heard the voice again—His voice.

"Not yet, not yet, the fruit has not bruised enough."

I stood frozen as a child before the cupboard, heart braying against my ribs. He was near. I could feel Him moving. Each step He took behind the walls loosed a draft of ancient air. I did not see Him—I rarely do now. Only the trailing echo, the glimpse of black silk slipping into doorways just before I arrive. Yet, His presence leaves behind evidence like ash marks on the ceiling.

A scrawl appeared on the wall behind the bureau.

"*Why did you leave the boy out?*"

It was written in that same fever-slashed script I found earlier in the nursery. I tried to rub it away with my sleeve, but it bled through the fabric, staining me. The ink was not ink. I know its smell. It was blood.

He refers, of course, to the murder. The other one. The one I have never spoken aloud. Not even in the memoir drafts. Not even to the doll, who has since become my companion in the darker hours. But He knows. Of course, He does. That night in the marsh, when I was only twelve. When the noble's son called me gutterborn. When the stone in my hand found his temple. When in fear, I gouged his throat with the penny knife I had stolen from his father just that night. I watched the body sink to as I rolled him into the canal.

I left that part out of *The Brothers of Gold*. I wrote of the poverty, the liaisons, the bitter laughter of wax-faced clients of work I never did, their breath always reeking of port. But not the boy. Never the boy.

He knows. He always knows.

The house has grown louder since I confessed the doll's name aloud: "Marion." As though baptizing her opened a channel. She whispers in dreams now. Sometimes, I wake with her in my hands, though I recall setting her far across the room.

She asks me to go below. "To where He waits."

This morning, I awoke to the manuscript scattered across the floorboards. Pages torn, ink smeared in loops and scratches,

I did not recall writing. But worst of all: a crimson fingerprint pressed upon the title page.

I checked my fingers. Clean.

I am no longer the sole author.

Hearth and Gallows is taking shape. The original is still here in spirit, but it has become something fungal. Spores were once prose. Every paragraph turns in on itself. Characters now weep from lesions. The father figure coughs up moths. The final scene is no longer a hanging—it is a feeding.

And yet, I do not wish to stop. I cannot.

My inkpot dried three days ago, yet my pen writes still. The red ink flows ceaselessly. I pricked my finger to examine it and found no wound. But I feel faint more often now—as though I'm being leeched.

Tonight, I returned to the parlour to burn the scattered pages— but He was already there.

No fanfare. No thunderclap.

He simply stood at the fireplace, a silhouette stitched of dusk, swaying in place as though caught in some drowned tide. His robes of pitch black moved with a wind that did not touch the drapes. His face—there is never a face. Only the suggestion of it beneath folds of shadowed cloth.

And then He spoke, as He does.

"There once was a man with a bleeding book, and he fed it his children. Not real ones, of course—he had none. But he tore pages from journals and stitched them into mouths.

His voice came as though spoken down a cathedral's throat, echoing not in the air but inside my own ribcage.

145

When the stories grew bored, he offered them tongues instead. They wanted more. So, he fed them eyes. They wept ink. He laughed. One night, the book asked for his name. He gave it

gladly. The next morning, there was no man. Only pages. Only

screams. Only truth."

He turned away before I could speak. Walked slowly toward the sealed trapdoor beneath the stairs. With every step, the walls groaned. I saw Him press a hand to the door—not to open it, but to bless it.

"Not yet. You're almost sweet enough."

And then He was gone.

The house is silent now. Too silent. Even the rats refuse to stir.

I no longer sleep with the lamp extinguished.

I leave this entry beneath the floorboard beneath my bed. Should I disappear, know this: the manor is not empty. It eats. And soon, I fear, it will be hungry again.

—*Wilde*

ENTRY XXVII: The Brothers of Mold

By Vattica Wilde

♪ ♪ ♪

I have set fire to the golden boy. His smile melts first. Then his tongue. The manuscript bubbles beneath my fingertips like fat in a pan, and I press deeper into the page until my knuckles stain with ink and blood.

The Brothers of Gold—that polished, hollow bauble of falseness—is gone. I have replaced it with the truth. With rot. With the smell of wet teeth and family dinners gone septic.

They will say I ruined it. That I defiled what little light I ever brought into the world. But it is not defilement to remove a mask. It is a revelation.

EXCERPT FROM THE BROTHERS OF MOLD

The younger brother, pale as curdled milk, crawled from the larder dragging his intestines like garlands. He sang a song of hunger in a voice stitched together from mouse squeaks and cracked church bells.

"You promised me marrow," he hissed to the elder, whose stomach gaped like a yawning library. "And instead, you gave me only stories."

The elder held up a severed hand and said, "But see! It is a metaphor for inheritance."

Then they dined on each other until the silence begged for company.

I remember when the first draft of Gold made me weep. Not for its beauty, but for the lie it made palatable. The way I had used language like a needle, suturing shut the mouth of the past.

But the mouth has split open again. Mold has burst from the spine. It grows between the lines, feasting on the pristine and the proud.

The younger brother—my brother—he is not golden. He never was. He was a squirming, frantic thing, so desperate to be loved, he let the world consume him and wore the teeth marks like medals. The elder was not wise. He was just quieter in his violence.

ANNOTATION – margin scrawled in crooked ink:

Rewrite the bones. Leave the skin behind. You know this is the version He prefers.

He comes to me at night, not to read, but to listen. He does not sit, nor breathe, nor judge. He leans from the shadows like a finger tapping a bruise, watching me bleed words that should have never healed in the first place.

His voice, when it comes, is damp:

"A lie, even lovely, cannot hide the rot. But a true story—told in bile and bone—will outlive God."

They held the birthday feast in a room lined with ribs. The younger brother wore a crown of spoiled grapes and was forced to eat his own name letter by letter.

The elder sliced poems from his skin and fed them to the guests, who wept and begged for more.

At the end, their mother arrived, pale and rotted, whispering, "What beautiful boys I've buried."

I once thought gold was incorruptible. But gold flakes. It blackens. It hides mold best. And in that mold lives the story— the true one, the one that drips, the one that devours.

COMMENTARY – lines crossed and rewritten repeatedly:

Am I the elder?

Is he?

Did I eat him, or did he die inside me?

What if we were never two? What if we were just a single scream split down the middle?

I have rewritten *The Brothers of Gold* line by line until I could no longer tell if I was revising or remembering.

The manuscript speaks back now. When I sleep, the paper curls like burned skin and mutters names I never knew I knew. I found a molar in the spine. A fly stitched into the paragraph break.

It is finished.

He says it's ready to be read. Or perhaps fed.

EXCERPT FROM THE BROTHERS OF MOLD

They returned to the cellar where stories ferment. There, beneath the dripping beams and mother's old shoes, the younger brother wrote his own ending:

"We were not gold.

We were never gold.

We were rot from the start.

Mold with names."

I mail the pages by firelight. I tie them with a lock of hair I don't remember cutting. The package stares at me. It hums.

He smiles when I'm done.

And from the far end of the hall, I hear my brother laugh.

But he's long since dead. Isn't he?

—V.

Entry XXVIII: God is a Critic

A Godless Day

I have returned to London.

The city has not missed me. I passed the grocer who once pinched his cap when I came by, but he looked through me like smoke. I moved through the old lanes like a phantom dressed in rust. I could smell the rot of fishmongers, the piss of horses, the cigarette burns on brick—and yet it was I who felt unclean. The manor had scabbed over me. Its silence was my skin now.

I came for only one reason—to return to the church I fled from all those entries ago.

Yes—that church.

The one with the narrow pews.

The one with the tilted eyes of saints.

The one with the statue of Mary, cold and stiff-lipped as a mother who's lost the will to weep.

It is precisely as I left it, and entirely changed.

I stood outside for a time, watching the gaslights melt in the high windows. The stones of its structure seemed less sacred than I remembered. More like bones pulled too tight over a ribcage. I didn't expect the doors to be open, but they were. Of course they were.

No one greeted me when I entered. No friar, no altar boy, no shuffling usher. Just dust motes suspended in that terrible hush churches wear like mourning veils.

She was still there.

Mary.

Still cloaked in blue and white, but her face has changed. No one moved her—I know this—but the corners of her eyes have sagged, her smile turned bitter. Time has made her cruel. Her hands that once folded in heavenly acceptance now looked as if they were bracing for something to strike her.

Her stone eyes seemed to follow me as I passed her.

I did not blink.

I wanted her to watch.

Further in, I took a pew. The same one I hid beneath when I was a boy, and that boy's voice broke into screaming. That same pew—the one with the scratch marks on the underside of the wood. I checked for them. They're still there.

A child sat three rows ahead.

Hair pale as bone.

Shoes too large.

He didn't move.

He didn't turn.

I didn't speak to him. I didn't need to.

I waited.

I do not know what I waited for. A priest? A sermon?

No. I waited for Him. But He did not come.

Something else did.

It began with the bells. I thought they tolled the hour, but the clock read nothing at all. Still, they rang—low and wet, like bones knocked together.

Then, a voice.

Not His. But something greater.

Vaster.

I could tell not where it came—not from the rafters, nor from within. It came from beneath language itself. It spoke through silence rather than breaking it.

You stitched your wounds with ink, and called the scar a story.

I froze.

You wrote a tomb, not a book.

Even the maggots are bored.

It spoke no title. No name. But it knew my name. My hands clenched, and I stared ahead at the altar. The boy still did not turn.

You made Him in your image, and called it suffering.

But He was never yours to invent.

I could feel the wood beneath me vibrating. Not from sound, but shame.

God—or some echo thereof—was condemning me.

And yet, nothing it said was untrue.

That was what hurt most.

> *You call it madness. I call it mediocrity.*

> *Even in ruin, you plagiarize your pain.*

That final line near broke me.

I tried to stand, but my knees shook. I wanted to scream. To answer. To fight— but I had no name for the thing that spoke.

No defense.

No passage of scripture.

No clever turn of phrase.

I fled before the final words could fall.

I don't know if the boy turned to watch me go.

I didn't look back at Mary either.

She had already turned away.

Now, I am back at the inn. Writing by lamplight, my clothes still stinking of holy stone and incense.

I feel no peace.

No catharsis.

Only a buzzing numbness beneath my ribs, like something lives there now.

Small.

Fluttering.

A moth.

A beetle.

A voice.

Was it God?

Was it *Him* in costume?

Was it guilt?

I leave this question unanswered.

I do not think I will return to London again.

The manor awaits.

And the manuscript is hungry.

 —*V.*

Entry XXIX: Throat of the House

Hollisby Manor

There is a throat in this house. Not a metaphor.

Not a flourish of language.

Not a poet's trick.

A throat.

Last night, I heard it—a groan passing through the walls like a swallowed sob. At first, I mistook it for the old wood settling, but this was no timber sigh. It was a voice of infrastructure: low and liquid, as if something deep within the manor were trying to speak in the language of pipe and pressure, gurgle and wheeze.

I followed it. How could I not? It was as if the house had finally taken notice of me. After all these weeks of feeding it stories—shedding ink and blood across its rooms—perhaps Hollisby had found something worth responding to. Me.

I crept barefoot through the corridors, the floorboards tender with rot. The air smelled of old mouths; damp and sour, like breath that had never seen daylight. It led me down to the belly of the house—past the library where He sometimes lingers in reflection, past the crumbling study where pages curl of their own accord, past even the boiler, which no longer hums but rasps.

Then, the groan again.

This time, not from beneath, but *behind* the walls.

A shudder. A wet rattle.

A sigh pulled through unseen organs.

I pressed my ear to the plaster.

I heard it unmistakably:

A breath.

Drawn-in. Struggling.

Phlegm-cloaked.

I whispered, "What are you trying to say?" It responded with a gulp.

Not words. Language has rules.

Hollisby—He—whatever god or parasite roosts here—has no use for grammar. He speaks in symbols. Stutters of sensation. A mosaic of rot and rhythm.

Still, I listened.

I wandered the halls with one ear pressed to wood and wallpaper, following the sound of a winded throat. I began to discern patterns. The hissing of the boiler echoed in sync with the creaks of the second-floor hall. The draft beneath the nursery door seemed to whistle with whispered syllables.

It's all connected. The plumbing. The framework. The bones of this place.

They are not architecture.

They are organs.

This house is alive.

No—alive is too generous a word.

It is *sustained*.

There is no heart, not in an mortal sense.

But there is a voice.

A throat.

And that is enough.

Today, I found what may be its mouth.

Behind a warped wardrobe in the servant's quarters: a grate I'd never noticed before. No draft. No chill. No obvious purpose. But as I leaned in, a hot, foul gust rose and curled into my sinuses like rotted milk.

I gagged.

And then—I heard Him.

Not as He usually comes. No apparition. No slow-motion drift through the parlour. No whispered annotations in the margins.

He spoke *through* the house.

His voice gurgled up the pipe like something congealed:

"The tongue was torn out, long ago. All it does now is swallow."

I dropped to my knees. I didn't know whether to laugh or retch.

"Speak, Vattica," he said.

"Feed it stories. Let it digest you." I asked what it wanted.

He said nothing more.

Only groaning. A peristaltic rhythm. Something behind the walls shifting. Squeezing.

I sat there for what may have been hours.

Journal open on my knees.

Pencil twitching.

I wrote nonsense. Drew spirals.

Fed the house syllables.

They won't nourish it.

But they may pacify its need to chew.

I returned to my quarters tonight to find my pages rewritten.

Not entirely.

Just words here and there.

Verbs inverted. Subjects switched.

A dream I'd described as "damp" was changed to "dampening."

A phrase I wrote—"The doll blinked again"—was crossed out.

Replaced with:

The doll waits.

Some edits are mine.

Some are jagged, unfamiliar.

They bleed through the paper like ink from a dying throat.

I've stopped crossing them out.

I let them stay.

Maybe He's editing.

Maybe the house is.

Maybe I was never the author.

Only the tongue.

And the tongue, as He said, is long gone.

I did not sleep.

I followed the voice again.

Deeper.

Past the nursery.

Past the library.

Past the cold pantry where meat has gone to worms.

Past the mirror that now reflects only the back of my head.

It led me to a wall in the cellar.

Stone. Not wood.

I pressed my hand to it.

Warm.

Not sun-warm. No.

Wet warmth.

Bodily.

As if the wall had circulation.

I pressed my ear to it.

I heard something.

Not groaning.

Chanting.

Wind dragged through a cathedral of lungs.

I cannot say what was said.

But I believe the house—or He—was praying.

I've begun to write sermons into the margins of my manuscript.

They are not mine.

I don't remember writing them.

But they're in my hand.

They repeat motifs from *The Brothers of Mold*:

The feast.

The bleeding mouth.

The golden marrow.

One line repeats over and over:

"The throat of the house is open. Feed it."

It frightens me how beautiful it sounds when I whisper it aloud.

I whispered it thirty-nine times this morning.

Then I blacked out.

When I awoke, there was blood on the stairs and ink in my mouth.

Tonight, I return to the mouth behind the grate.

I bring with me pages—torn, scribbled, sacrificial.

If the house is a throat, then I will be its heretic choir.

Let the house swallow.

Let the house speak.

Let it sermon its way into the marrow of the world. Let me be the tongue it lost so long ago.

—*V.*

166

ENTRY XXX: Reflections in Gaslight

Broken

It is a cruel thing to walk backward in one's mind—where the past does not sit idle, but reaches forth, clawing its way into the present like a fever rising beneath the skin.

I did not intend to remember.

But the walls have begun to murmur.

And I, ever the obedient listener, cannot look away from the places they reveal.

I was twelve. Perhaps thirteen.

A boy-shaped ghost scuttling along the cobbled arteries of France.

My bones were too slight to cast real shadows.

My presence, soft enough to be mistaken for silence itself.

The gaslights overhead—yellow and wheezing—did not illuminate me.

They only carved deeper contours in the hollows of my cheeks, made my existence more secret than it already was.

There was a night.

A night like a bruise.

It rained in that particular way France does best, where the

air turns viscous and everything smells of soot, horse piss, and rot.

I remember being pulled inside by a gloved hand—silk, not leather.

That detail I cannot forget.

The softness of the glove.

How unlike a hand it felt.

How much worse for it.

I watched with rot in my stomach as he produced a key.

Burnished brass, dangling from a thin chain. The number 414 branded within.

We climbed two flights of stairs in a narrow inn off Whitechapel Road.

The hallway bent oddly, as though the building had grown crooked with age and shame.

It smelled of mold and wood that had never known sunlight.

I had not yet begun to assign emotion to scent—but if I had, it would have been despair.

He did not speak. Not at first.

Only the sound of the key entering the lock.

The slow click.

The whisper of that glove as he gestured me inside.

The room was too warm—like the breath of someone feverish.

A single oil lamp burned on a side table, casting our shapes in long, skeletal streaks across the walls.

There was a crucifix above the bed.

Always, a crucifix.

He was a man with a mustache too neatly groomed, his suit damp with rain, his eyes empty of anything but function.

His glove slid along my cheek as if smoothing out a wrinkle in fabric.

I remember his scent—ink and port wine—and beneath that: something medicinal.

A doctor, perhaps. Or a man pretending to be one.

He asked me to smile.

I did.

And then he wept.

That was the part I could not understand.

The part that never fit the rest of the scene.

He wept as he undid his collar, as he placed his gloves beside the lamp.

He wept so quietly I wondered if he even knew. He was doing it at all.

It was not sadness. Not guilt.

Something deeper. Older.

Like mourning.

He called me by another name.

I did not ask whose.

The act itself was brief.

I had learned early how to absent myself from my body.

Dissociation is a kind of artistry—a vanishing trick more elaborate than anything Houdin ever performed.

But afterward, when he asked to hold me, when he whispered Latin and some broken version of prayer—it was then I felt the true weight of the room.

The crucifix.

It presses still, against the inside of my skull, like a forgotten bruise.

I left with a coin wrapped in a handkerchief silk, damp from his palm.

The sky had cleared—slightly.

The gaslights flickered.

My shoes had holes.

I think my hands trembled.

I told myself it was the cold.

Now, decades later, I pass a mirror in this godforsaken

manor and see something else in my reflection:

A boy still gloved in silence.

Still obedient.

Still trying to find a shape that is not aching.

There is a part of me that wonders:

Did He exist even then?

Was that man simply another face worn by a darker thing?

The glove was too soft.

The crying too still.

The number 414 too persistent.

The room should not matter.

But it does.

I had not thought of that night for years.

Not once.

Not through the clamor of literary success, nor through the echoing decline.

But now, the manor breathes in time with memories I did not give permission to rise.

And I am beginning to suspect that what I wrote in *The Brothers of Gold* was not fiction softened by metaphor—but truth I had no other way of telling.

There was no love in that encounter.

No transaction of tenderness.

Only proof that I was malleable.

Breakable.

And very much for sale.

Now, in this decaying manor where every mirror tilts its face away from mine,

I see 414 scratched faintly on a beam above the hearth.

A trick of the light, perhaps. Or perhaps not.

He has found me again.

Or maybe He never left.

—*Vattica Wilde*

Entry XXXI: The Storyteller's Debt

Hollisby Manor, December 19th

A tale visited me in the hours between dusk and fever—when the mind simmers, and the ink in the bottle pulses like a throat trying to speak. Whether it was whispered to me by Him or found like a worm at the core of my mind's fruit, I cannot say. But I must write it.

It is the story of a man who gave everything for a story that would never end. And it is not fiction.

No, not anymore.

"The Tale of the Bleeding Quill"

(as best I remember it)

There was once a man whose name had been eaten by time. Let us call him only the Storyteller. He lived in a crumbling village where the sun never rose properly and the church bell rang with a note like a throat clearing before a lie. The people were drab and clay-colored, trudging through their days with cracked mouths and half-formed prayers.

But the Storyteller—they adored him. He spun tales that made their colorless world throb briefly with life. Kings who tore their crowns in half to rule beside their shadows. Children whose teeth sang when they smiled. Rivers that flowed backwards to unlive old sins.

The villagers clutched these stories like rosaries. They did not eat them; they worshiped them.

One day, the Storyteller ran dry. He awoke with nothing—no voices, no visions, no shapes in the soup. His mind was barren, like the field of graves behind the chapel. And the villagers grew anxious. They came to his window with gifts: rotted apples, stitched dolls, and butchered birds—all hoping to inspire him.

But no words came.

That night, he wandered into the forest, where the trees stood like bent spines. He screamed into the darkness, cursed the gods of ink, and wept like the last boy on earth.

Then a voice answered.

It was not loud, nor cruel, nor sweet. It simply was, and it spoke through the wind and rot:

"You wish for a story that never ends." He nodded.

"Then trade with Me."

The Storyteller, half-mad with longing, carved a vow into his chest with the edge of his penknife. He offered his soul, his tongue, and the last dream he'd ever have. The voice accepted.

And so, the story began.

He returned to the village and wrote. Oh, how he wrote. Day and night, on parchment, stone, and flesh. He wrote on the walls of the bakery and the bell tower's bones. His fingers bled. His eyes went pale. But the stories never stopped.

He told tales that made widows weep into the mouths of their lovers. Tales that caused the crops to sprout red and the cattle to walk backward into their own mothers. The villagers became addicted. They stopped praying. They built him a throne of ink-drenched books.

But they did not see what grew beneath the pages.

Each word he wrote cost something. His tongue blackened. His fingertips fell off, one by one. And the stories began to speak back. Names he did not invent. Deaths he did not design. Whole chapters he could not remember writing.

One day, the villagers found him nailed to his own desk, hands pierced by the quill, still writing. He had scribbled his final words in a language no one recognised. When they tried to burn the manuscript, it did not burn. When they buried it, the earth refused to close.

It is said the manuscript still writes itself.

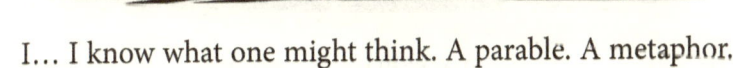

I... I know what one might think. A parable. A metaphor. A madman's myth to explain the pit into which he willingly crawled.

But I see now that I did not write The Brothers of Gold. I uncovered it.

And now, I have rewritten it into its proper form—The Brothers of Mold. This tale—the true one—climbs out of the marrow of my bones. It decays as it breathes. It is alive, and what is more—it is hungry.

The story consumes me in turn. Each draft more intimate than the last. I smell it when I sleep. I wake with pulp under my nails, and I do not know if it is paper or flesh.

It has given me visions. He, of course, was watching over my shoulder, correcting phrasing with fingers made of flies. He laughed when I wrote the new scene of Elias peeling gold from his gums. He made me underline the passage where Sol drinks spoiled wine and whispers, "I deserve to rot."

"Add more teeth," He scrawled once.

I obliged.

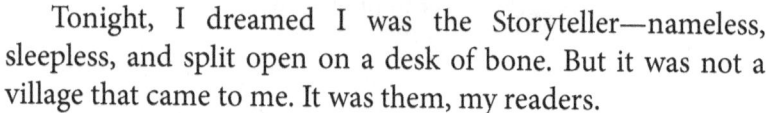

Tonight, I dreamed I was the Storyteller—nameless, sleepless, and split open on a desk of bone. But it was not a village that came to me. It was them, my readers.

Them, standing in the doorway of my thoughts, their faces blank, their eyes chewing through each sentence as if it were bread in a starving man's mouth.

They will finish this story for me, won't they?

My hands hurt. The ink won't wash off anymore. It stains my tongue, my teeth, the whites of my eyes. I have tried to burn the manuscript, but it only weeps. I buried a chapter in the woods and found it by my bedside the next morning, now titled Confession II: Vattica's Creed in handwriting not my own.

And I—I am changing. My thoughts come in pairs, sometimes in voices. I see the boy from the pews walking the halls. He asks me if the story will ever end. I do not answer.

Because I know now: it won't. That is the debt.

—V.W.

Entry XXXII: Rotten Milk and Maggots

❦ ❦ ❦

The hunger returns—not as ache, but as hatred.

The pantry has turned against me.

I opened the cupboard this morning, and the bread bled—a thick pink syrup weeping from its center, like a womb sliced prematurely. The milk curdled before my eyes, bloating the bottle until the glass screamed and split—maggots already swimming in the spoiled sea. They floated in procession like pale priests; their little bodies bent in prayer. And I—I stood witness to this sacrament of decay.

The egg, cracked upon the pan, hissed like a serpent and spat blood. "There are no chickens here," I whispered, though the house did not answer. Not with words. Only with stench.

He is trying to starve me.

He, with his ink-blot eyes and candlewax limbs.

He who whispers scripture through the cracks in my cutlery drawer.

He who watches me count crumbs.

I chewed on a crust of what was once rye, but it tasted of mold—and sermon. I spat it out, only to find my teeth left impressions in the wood of the table. My tongue is changing. Or perhaps the wood is softer now. Swollen with secrets.

What does one eat when the house revolts?

Ink.

He leaves it everywhere—pools in the corners of rooms I don't remember entering, dots on the wallpaper shaped like alphabets never spoken aloud. And now: a goblet, placed neatly beside my writing desk, filled to its brim.

I toasted no one. I drank it anyway.

It burned—oh, how it burned—like swallowing shadow and gulping the echo of a bell never rung. It tasted of guilt. Of manuscripts I never finished. Of boys I kissed and forgot. Of my brother's silent screams as the river took him. Of Mary in the church with the broken hands. Of all things I buried under prose and called fiction.

I ate ink on toast today.

At first, it repulsed me—but then, there was a kind of beauty to it. A black elegance. The bread held the lines like a page. And when I bit into it, the words bled into my mouth. This is the body, I thought. This is the text made flesh.

He laughed from the walls—not loud, not cruel, just...

Amused. Like a father watching his child play with knives.

I could feel his fingers tracing along my spine.

I found a message scrawled in beetle trails on the wall above the stove:

"You taste better hungry."

It is no longer clear who the author is.

Is it I who writes in blood, and eats his ink?

Or He, who leaves sermons in sour milk and feeds me prophecy by maggot?

The lines are blurring. I hunger still.

Tonight, I will try buttering my journal pages.

If I am to be consumed, let it be by my own hand.

—V.

ENTRY XXXIII: 414 Once More

Hollisby Manor, Here on the Night of Rot

There was a room in France I've spent a lifetime trying to forget.

A room numbered 414.

I know this now because I have carved the number into the wood with my own teeth—twelve marks slashed in bone and splintered oak.

I know because the memory rose at me like a tide, dragging me back into an agony I buried beneath polite fiction.

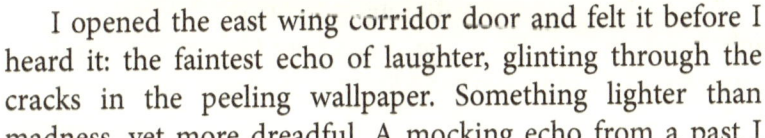

I opened the east wing corridor door and felt it before I heard it: the faintest echo of laughter, glinting through the cracks in the peeling wallpaper. Something lighter than madness, yet more dreadful. A mocking echo from a past I dare not reclaim.

And then, pinned to the wall beside me, I saw it—"*414*"—etched in trembling pencil, as if someone had once needed to remember where they lay their head. Or perhaps to remind themselves how they lost it.

I fled. Of course, I fled. The corridors twisted beneath my feet; the candle guttered as though chasing a phantom. But the number clung to the back of my skull, pulsing like a warning.

I returned to my study, heart hammering, fingers slick with sweat. I tried to write it down, to banish it with ink, but the pen lurched in my hand, stained itself red and black, and spelled

414 on the page when I did not will it so.

And then I remembered.

I was twelve? Certainly not yet thirteen—too young to know the breadth of shame, too old to be spared its sting. I wore ragged coats and borrowed shoes. My mouth had learned the taste of coin before it ever knew the taste of bread.

Room 414 was a servant's garret above Mrs. Haverstock's bawdy house. A place behind a worn tapestry, behind a door without a lock, where I learned to sell my body to rich men and women who pretended tenderness but only sought my theft— my youth, my voice, my last shred of dignity.

The bed there was narrow, the mattress a sack of feathers and lice. The wallpaper peeled in curling strips, revealing obscene portraits of cherubs reeking of mildew, mocked with a crucifix. And I—skin raw with longing—lay beneath cracked gaslight, reciting lines from *The Brothers of Gold* as though it were prayer, as though story could save me from the ache in my belly.

I blocked it out. How could I recall bargains made in lust and desperation? The keys I slipped into my pocket when my exploiters slept. The soft sobs I swallowed in the dark. The time I hurt someone so badly, I thought their breath would never return.

I left that life behind. I tried to bury it beneath applause, beneath ink, beneath success.

I called it a different story. But stories are debts.

Tonight, the number returned—not as memory, but as

command. 414. Three digits like a scar. A confession.

I found the beam in my bedroom—the one running diagonally beneath the plaster, hidden by rotten wallpaper. My teeth found a gap, my jaw clamped, and I began to gnaw.

4—first mark, shallow, tasting of wood.

1—second mark, deeper, as my thumb bled.

4—third mark, ragged, echoing the tears I never shed.

The taste of oak and blood swirled on my tongue. I tasted youth and shame and the stink of that room. I tasted the hands that touched me, the coins that bought me, the lies I told myself so I might smile afterward.

I write this through a haze of pain. My jaw throbs. My mouth tastes of rotting wood.

Why did I come back here? Why did I invite this memory? Because He beckoned me, I suspect. Because this house—this living mass—hungrily collects confessions like beetles gather carrion. It devours what we bury, and when we think ourselves safe, it returns us to the banquet.

I remember now the first time I heard it in that 414 garret:

the whisper in the walls. Not a draft, not the scurrying of rats, but a voice so low I thought it was my own thoughts echoing:

"This room knows every lie you've ever told."

I was twelve. I could not name sin, but I felt it like a stone in my gut. I covered my ears, but the stone stayed.

Now, I see how it begins and ends the same way: whisper, confession, bone.

I have whispered to this manor my entire life—my failures, my shame, my ecstasies—and it always replies in kind, fed back to me as dread.

So, I carved my number. My beginning. My sin. 4-1-4.

Because tonight, the house waits once more at that number.

Like London, I will return to France no more. But the echo of 414 will follow me, trailing from one room to the next, a funeral march in timber beats.

And I—ink-blinded, blood-blasted, mind rent—will not outrun that echo.

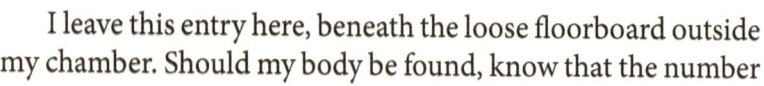

I leave this entry here, beneath the loose floorboard outside my chamber. Should my body be found, know that the number will be there, carved twice: once in oak, once in bone.

—*Vattica*

ENTRY XXXIV: My Soul to Keep

I do not know the hour, nor the day—only that the house has gone quiet again.

There is no breath in the walls tonight.

The pipes have hushed their hymn.

Even He, who once hummed beneath the floorboards, has gone still.

I write this from the same chair where I began. The ink is not ink. It has never been. The blood clots in the nib now, as if reluctant to leave me. I press harder. I carve my words, now. Carve them into the page the way I carved 414 into the beam— yes, I remember now. That room. That number. The boy who was not quite a boy, and the man who paid not with coin, but with silence.

I am still in that room.

I never left. The manor is only a continuation. The mattress only got larger. The ghosts only got louder.

The paper curls at the edges like burnt skin. I can smell it— charred leather and stale milk. I am not hungry anymore. He feeds me in other ways.

There is no more need for fiction.

The story is the truth now.

And the truth is a knife.

I saw my reflection this morning.

It did not look like me. It was a man made of mildew and dripping ink, and he smiled at me with my teeth.

He wore my eyes like baubles.

He reached out and pressed his palm to the mirror.

I did the same.

But mine was cold.

His was warm.

There is something wrong with the ceiling.

It sags. It breathes. It knows I am beneath it.

The doll has begun to whisper again.

She has taken a name, though I will not write it. Names give life. I dare not grant her that.

She warned me not to open the manuscript again.

I did.

I always do.

It rewrites itself while I sleep. Entire passages I don't remember drafting now crawl across the margins. Sermons from He. Retellings of things I should not have seen.

I found a page soaked in something slick. It smelled like the boiler room.

It smelled like her.

The one I left behind.

The one who asked me to stay.

My handwriting is changing. It grows thinner, more precise. His influence, perhaps.

Or maybe I have simply become more myself.

There was a sound just now.

Not the pipes. Not the house.

The mail slot.

It opened. It's embedded in the far wall—where once there was only peeling of wallpaper. I never saw it before. It should not be there.

It is just wide enough for the manuscript. He is ready.

A confession, then, before the end.

I killed a man when I was young.

No, younger than that.

He paid me in silver and called me brilliant before he bled.

It was not guilt that drove me to write *The Brothers of Gold*.

It was pride.

And now that gold has tarnished. It flakes off like scabs. Beneath it?

Flesh.

Rot.

The truth.

This is the final story.

There are no readers.

Only witnesses.

And He watches now.

He is closer than breath.

His shadow covers the door.

I can see it from the corner of my eye.

He waits for the final line.

He always does.

He is patient.

He may be kind.

—Vattica

ENTRY XXXV: Confession II: Vattica's Creed

[Editor's Note: Written in Vattica's hand, the ink jagged with trembling loops and blotted corners. A final, fevered sermon to the self.]

I have bled this house dry.

I have wept into its walls.

I have given it every word I own, and it still asks for more.

So be it. Let me become ink.

He watches me write now.

Not over the shoulder as before—no, behind the eyes. His silence is louder than any voice I've ever known. I once thought I feared Him because He was otherworldly. I was wrong.

I fear Him because He is me, only honest.

And so, I begin this last act, not as Vattica Wilde the failed author, nor Vattica Wilde the fool with stars in his teeth.

But Vattica Wilde, penitent, ready to be published by Him.

This is not an entry. It is a creed.

I. *On the Ink Beneath My Skin*

The first lie I ever told was a sentence I believed. I called it *The Brothers of Gold*, and the world kissed my name for it.

But there was rot in that book, hiding beneath metaphor and symmetry. I wrapped my truth in silk and stitched shut its mouth.

He has shown me the mouth again.

My fingers ache from rewriting. The ink turned red days ago. My quill, if you can believe it, was once a rib. Not mine. A child's. I found it behind the nursery wall, wrapped in lace and birth tape.

They used to call me a craftsman. A weaver of tales. But I am only a butcher now. The musings of He is a wound. An autopsy with no cadaver. I write not to be read, but to be found.

II. *On the Number 414*

The number came again in last night's fever.

I scratched it into a beam with my teeth.

But I remember now.

It was the room I would rent by the hour when I was too young to know how deep loneliness could dig.

Room 414.

Red carpet. Greasy lamp. Always smelled of old wine and lilac piss.

It was there that I sold myself, not for coin, but for recognition. I wanted someone to say, "I see you." They never did.

They only took.

I buried that room in *The Brothers of Gold*. I turned it into a gilded parlour with sunlight and honor and clever dialogue.

He made me remember what it truly was.

And so, I carved it into the manor's rib. Let it scream.

III. *A Prayer for the Dead Things Inside Me*

To the boy with blood between his legs:

I forgive you.

To the man who ran from the church, who couldn't look at Mary's eyes as they followed him down the aisle:

I forgive you.

To the mouth that kissed the pastor's son and liked the taste of guilt:

I forgive you.

To the child who pushed another child down into the canal and told no one:

I cannot forgive you.

But He might.

He might, if you give Him everything.

IV. *The Mail Slot That Should Not Exist*

There is a slit in the stone wall by the cellar door.

It was not there yesterday.

It is brass and old, and its hinges whisper.

It hums at night. A low, coiling sound—like a throat clearing before it speaks.

I touched it this morning. My fingers came away warm.

That is where the manuscript must go.

Not to a publisher.

Not to the world.

But to Him.

He, who sees the truth beneath every tidy sentence.

He, who watches from the mirror and behind the teeth.

He, who whispered the first line into my ear as I lay paralyzed in bed all those nights ago.

"God is dead," He said. "And the story killed Him."

So, I will give Him my story. Not to resurrect God, but to bury Him deeper.

V. *A Manifesto of Madness*

What is literature but sacrament?

What is authorship but blasphemy, inked?

I have lied through every chapter.

I have disfigured saints and scrubbed dirt from corpses to make them palatable.

No more.

This is not a story.

This is not a confession.

This is not a cry for help.

This is my submission.

My skin is lined with rejected metaphors.

My teeth gnash through metaphor like meat.

My soul is footnoted.

And when the critics come, they will say it was "too much." They will call it indulgent. Disgusting. Unreadable.

Good.

Let them choke on every syllable. Let them cough up my name like phlegm.

Because I was not made to be adored. I was made to be devoured.

VI. *He Has Begun to Read Me Aloud*

I hear Him now.

At night, beneath the boards, He reads the manuscript aloud.

His voice is slow and wet, like something chewing vowels.

He mispronounces nothing.

He laughs when I write something false. He sighs when I write something true.

He is my editor. My publisher. My mirror.

And tomorrow, I will slide this book to Him. Through the slit. Into the warm mouth of the wall.

And He will read it in full.

And He will decide what to do with me.

VII. *Vattica's Creed I, Vattica Wilde*

I do hereby offer myself,

word and wound,

sentence and sin,

to He who whispers in rot and ink.

I do not seek salvation.

I seek publication.

May my flesh be margins.

May my thoughts be preface.

May my bones be the spine upon which He binds.

Let this manuscript be my body.

Let this house be my press.

Let this madness be my legacy.

I am no longer writing this book.

I am being written by it.

And I accept.

With trembling hands and a shattered tongue, I sign my name not with ink.

Not with the life giving blood of a creative mind.

But with what's left of my soul.

I write with rot.

I write with what is left of my shattering.

Vattica Wilde
Author of He

ENTRY XXXVI: HE

He is watching me now. He wants me to hang.

He wants me to

[The line trails off. There is no closing signature.]

Postscript I: Discovery

Editor's Note, Benedict Lowre

The manuscript arrived not at my door but in the corner of an archival crate misfiled and nearly rotted through. According to surviving records, it had been deposited at the offices of Wexley & Sons, a modest Victorian publisher best known for sentimental paperbacks and monographs on temperance.

They never published it.

The note paperclipped to the ribbon-bound volume reads only:

"Unsolicited. Unsellable. Possibly dangerous. We will not be taking this further."

The handwriting is prim and tight. A dated flourish curls at the end, but no name accompanies it. There's no indication that anyone at Wexley & Sons read beyond the first few pages. The manuscript was boxed and filed as "Speculative Fiction (Unpublished)," then buried beneath receipts, contracts, and brittle review clippings.

It remained there for nearly two centuries.

I discovered it during a routine archival transfer, buried among correspondence between minor literary figures and their abandoned second drafts. It was miscategorized, listed under the wrong Wilde—someone's careless scrawl mistook V. Wilde for Oscar.

I almost passed it by.

But I opened it.

And now I cannot seem to close it again.

The manuscript is... unwell. The ink runs in places. Some pages are smeared with what looks like dried blood; others are punctured, as though someone had bitten the paper. Dates seem incorrect, and the last third is scrawled in a hand far more jagged than the first. The voice shifts from lucid despair to outright mania. It's a journal, yes—but also a story, a sermon, a suicide note, a confession, a hallucination, a plea.

It is The Musings of He by Vattica Wilde—failed novelist, societal exile, and, as far as records indicate, a man who disappeared without a trace sometime in 1837—until now.

I could have stopped there. I should have. But compulsion is a powerful thing. Wilde speaks of a place—a house—again and again. He calls it Hollisby Manor, though no such name appears on any official registry.

It was, however, mentioned in a single letter, misfiled among Wilde's surviving correspondence. A crumbling envelope, sealed with black wax. The letter within made only one claim:

"He's still in the boiler room. I never opened the door. I still hear Him breathing."

I made the journey last winter.

The manor, as it turns out, is real. But it is not what you expect.

More in Postscript II: The Visit.

Postscript II: The Visit

Hollisby Manor was not marked on any modern map, not even the satellite ones. I triangulated its approximate location from Vattica Wilde's scattered references, outdated county borders, and the single surviving parcel map from 1794. Even so, it took me three hours by car, another forty minutes on foot, and an unkind scramble through a fence choked with briar to find it.

And there it was.

Not a haunted cathedral of grotesquerie as Wilde described, but something more pitiful: sagging bricks, ivy devouring its face, a manor too small to ever have been noble and too large to be forgotten this long. Hollisby sits like a mouth that has forgotten how to speak. The chimneys lean. The windows sag. Whatever coat of arms once adorned its gables has long been weathered to a faceless oval of moss and lichen. I almost laughed when I first saw it. I was braced for madness. Instead, I found disrepair.

There was no lock on the front door—just swollen wood and rusted hinges. I should have brought gloves. It took both shoulders to budge it open. The inside smelled of mildew and something older. Not rot. Not decay. Time itself.

No walls bled. No voices called. But silence had weight here—terrible and low, like something crouched in the corners waiting to see if I'd flinch.

I found the foyer nearly intact. Dust had softened every edge, but the layout matched Wilde's description almost exactly: a split stairwell branching left and right, a chandelier hanging low enough to threaten the scalp of any tall guest, and the faint remnants of once-rich wallpaper, its pattern now curled and fading to green-gray.

To the left was the drawing room.

Wilde wrote of this space with fervor—how the wallpaper would undulate, how portraits would shift when looked at too long. I found nothing of the sort. The portraits had been removed or vandalized. Only rectangular ghosts of discoloration on the walls remained. One painting—perhaps a landscape or a hunting party—lay face down on the floor, frame splintered and canvas torn straight through. No signs of violence. Just age. Collapse. The fireplace was cold. A few scraps of scorched paper remained inside, but I didn't attempt to read them.

To the right: the parlour.

The furnishings here had fared better. A settee upholstered in fraying maroon velvet, a tea table with two mismatched chairs. Some China, still in the cabinet. A broken teacup on the rug, its handle resting nearby like a severed ear. Wilde claimed that this room once hosted séances. He wrote of voices rising from the drainpipes, of chairs that rearranged themselves, of an invisible woman who refused to sit anywhere but the third chair from the fire. All I saw was a neglected room with fading décor and an odd draft.

The air in Hollisby does not move like ordinary air. It lingers. It tastes of stone and forgotten breath.

Upstairs, I found the nursery.

I followed a trail of warped floorboards and a narrow hallway whose wallpaper had peeled in such perfect strips that they resembled hanging tongues. The nursery had no windows—just like Wilde said. The light filtered in only through a slatted vent in the upper wall, casting the room in a strange, jail-like grid of shadows.

The doll was there.

Just as he described her.

Porcelain, cracked. Missing an eye. Her little dress stained at the collar. She had been propped up against the baseboard beneath the vent, her arms folded primly in her lap. A child's chair beside her had rotted in place. I did not touch her.

Other things in the room struck me with similar eerie mundanity. There was a bookshelf of rotted spines, most illegible. A mobile made of pressed tin moons, tangled in cobwebs. One tiny shoe in the far corner, stiff with mold. The cradle had been pushed against the wall and was empty.

Wilde had written of whispers in this room, of the doll's eye following him, of the sensation that a small cold hand had taken his own. I felt nothing like that. Only a strange sorrow, heavy as velvet.

I descended next into the kitchen and scullery, now entirely collapsed. Brick had fallen through one end of the ceiling and left the whole area choked with detritus. Black mildew coated the walls where pipes had ruptured and spilled years of rainwater and rot. Wilde's "vision of a slaughterer's chamber" was nowhere in sight. Just a ruined mess of stone, rusted fixtures, and hollow cupboards gnawed by time.

I continued out back.

The garden.

It did exist, though barely. Most of it was a tangle of vine and bramble, but the outlines were there: a curved path of stone, the remnants of a fountain, a wrought-iron bench whose legs had sunk several inches into the earth. Wilde had described the garden as a "temple of unnatural geometry," a place where

"flowers bled ink" and where "the sun never fully reached."

I found only a forgotten plot overrun by nature. Nothing bloomed. Nothing moved. The sun reached just fine. The only vaguely unsettling object was a rusted trellis, wrapped so tightly with dead vine that it seemed to shudder when I brushed past it—but even that could be blamed on wind.

Behind the garden, past a lopsided gate of cracked iron, I found what Wilde called the Servants' Path—a narrow, descending trail that hugged the outer edge of the house's foundation. It led down to a secondary entrance, half submerged, which I took to be the cellar.

This, I suspected, would be the worst of it.

And in some ways, it was.

The boiler room.

The door stuck. I pried it open with a crowbar I had intended to use on the front door. The hinges screamed.

The room beyond is nearly featureless. A black, iron drum dominates the space like a waiting tomb. Soot crusts the walls. The air is still. No buzzing, no breath. Just that awful quiet.

I told myself I was alone. Then I saw it.

A body.

A figure slumped in the corner, collapsed beside the cold iron. Skin—what remained of it—shriveled over bone like dried fruit left in the sun too long. The clothing was shredded, velvet rotted to threads. One hand clutched a bundle of pages, now fused together by time, soot, and blood.

The other hand was gone; bones scattered several feet away. The jaw was slack, open in a final gasp.

I did not touch it. I had no authority to retrieve him, no explanation to offer.

But I know in my gut what I found.

Vattica Wilde.

Died there. Or something that used to be him.

He wrote of seeing himself dead before he died, of a figure mirroring his every movement from a place "beneath the hearth." But I found no doppelgänger, no shadow twin. Only a corpse with Wilde's general description, curled in death against the boiler he once feared.

What I can't explain—what I won't explain—is this: as I turned to leave, I passed a narrow doorway that led to the rear wall. Just above the baseboard, a small brass slot had been carved into the plaster.

A mail slot.

It was not rusted. Not broken. It looked new.

And inside, wedged just barely into its opening, was a torn scrap of paper in familiar, frantic handwriting:

"He said you would come."

And yet I must emphasize: nothing else about the visit was remotely supernatural.

No doors slammed of their own accord. No lights flickered. I saw no phantoms. I heard only wind. I do not believe I was in danger. Nor do I believe the house has any particular interest in me.

It is just a place now. An old, sad place.

Its horrors, if ever they lived, have long since dried up.

It is not haunted. It is merely hollow.

A hollow that once contained a man who desperately wanted to be believed.

Postscript III: The Scholars

Collected Notes from "The Wilde Symposium,"
Cambridge, 2022

Excerpted from panel discussion, "Madness, Manuscript, and Myth: Interpreting Vattica Wilde"

Dr. Thomas Reed (Professor of Literary Psychiatry):

"It's not uncommon for posthumously discovered works to reveal the author's decline. Wilde's Musings of He, however, is something different. The structure is coherent—deliberate, even elegant—yet the content spirals into psychosis. That tension is what makes it so difficult to diagnose. He wasn't writing gibberish. He was building a system of belief. A theology of madness. Or at the very least, a very convincing imitation of one."

Dr. Anika Dhuval (Cultural Archivist):

"The Hollisby Journal—what we now refer to as Musings of He—was dismissed for over a century. Misfiled, mislabeled, possibly purposefully avoided. The marginalia alone reads like religious ecstasy. His obsession with 'He' parallels early Christian mystics, but it's also reminiscent of schizophrenia. It's a collision of the sacred and the symptomatic."

Dr. Harold Lyn (Folklorist):

"I don't believe Wilde invented 'Him.' Similar entities appear in rural English folklore as early as the 13th century—cloaked figures, whispering in sleep, delivering strange directives. What Wilde did, perhaps for the first time, was give it authorship. He made 'He' a collaborator."

Dr. Louisa Grey (Historian):

"Wilde was not a well man. That's not speculation— that's fact. But dismissing the manuscript as pure delusion is irresponsible. There are elements we cannot explain. Certain symbols in the manuscript predate Wilde. The boiler room sketch? Matches layouts from Victorian sacrificial cults. And the doll—her specific construction was never common in England. It suggests outside influence. Perhaps... ancient. Perhaps imagined. But not accidental."

Audience Question:

"But what about the boy in the pews? Did Wilde fabricate him, too?"

Dr. Reed:

"I'm not convinced he was ever real. But Wilde certainly was haunted by him. Sometimes guilt takes a form. Sometimes grief writes back."

Postscripts IV: The Archivist's Margin

Interoffice Memo: Department of Special Collections, Internal Use Only

Filed under: Unprocessed / Provenance Uncertain / Wilde, Vattica (?) —Box 3

Author: Dr. Ellory Finch

Date: [Undated]

Clearance: Internal Circulation —Do Not Reproduce

Without Supervisor Approval

To whomever is next assigned this parcel of mystery and mildew:

I hesitate to even refer to it as a "manuscript," though that is what it appears to be. It arrived in Box 3 of the Wilde Subcollection during the re-shelving of our Special Collections overflow, bundled incorrectly between a sheaf of Victorian sermon notes and a half-charred copy of Mors Aurea: Essays on the Beautiful Death. I mention the latter only because it wasn't in the box's original contents list. Neither was the volume.

That discrepancy is the first anomaly.

The second is that none of us filed it.

I've been with this department for sixteen years. We don't lose track of acquisitions without notice. There is no accession number, no curator's initials, and no form F-19 for unverified literary ephemera. I queried everyone in Processing, Reference, and Collections Management. No one admits to touching it. No one admits to opening it. One of our student assistants claims the box arrived already sealed, with no return label.

I believe them.

The third anomaly—if it can be called that—is something I would not normally put in writing. I will speak plainly, because this will almost certainly never leave internal circulation: one page was not where I left it.

I do not mean it was misfiled or that it shifted in transit. I

mean—I personally placed the folio on page 237, if the internal numerals can be trusted, beneath the fold of the front matter to preserve the edge from further flaking. I placed a slip between the folios. I initialed it.

When I returned the following morning, the page was no longer there. It was in the back third of the volume, between what appear to be Vattica Wilde's last two entries. No slip. No initials. The paper looks identical to the rest, with the same weight and oxidation, but the change is undeniable.

I did not move it.

That is all I will say on the matter.

Content-wise, the volume is eclectic. "Musings of He" (a title scrawled in uncertain graphite over a torn half-title) reads part memoir, part theological tract, part fiction—or perhaps none of those. Wilde, if he is indeed the author, exhibits periods of coherence punctuated by disintegration, both linguistic and psychological. There are signs of ink degradation consistent with long-term exposure to damp, as well as a few pages marred by what looks suspiciously like human blood. One of our conservation team declined to test it.

She cited "a gut feeling."

I do not say this with any intention to embellish. We work in archives. We handle worse. There is nothing inherently haunted about decay.

But I will note this: every person who has handled the manuscript, from interns to supervisors, has returned it to me within a day, citing discomfort, nausea, or an overwhelming sense of fatigue. Completing a full read through seems begrudging.

It has now sat in my office for forty-three days.

I have completed two full passes and part of a third.

I cannot say why.

Part of it is professional obligation. But another part, a quieter and less noble part, suspects that the manuscript wants something—not in the supernatural sense, but in the same way a disused room sometimes seems to wait for a visitor. You know the feeling. Most of us have been librarians too long to pretend spaces do not shape behavior.

The text, if authentic, is significant. Wilde was believed to have vanished in 1838 without a trace. This manuscript—assuming the dating is accurate—would have been written between 1836 and 1838. That alone warrants investigation.

Yet nothing about it feels verifiable.

I've attempted to triangulate the place names Wilde references—"Hollisby Manor," "Millgate Hollow," "the Old Reverence." None appear on official maps. The closest match, in the 1794 parcel register, is a deconsecrated hunting estate referred to locally as "the Hollow House." I've forwarded the map to the Editor for further research. I do not wish to go looking for myself.

As for disposition, I recommend neither destruction nor exhibition.

Let it pass quietly to the Editor's desk. If she finds something of note within, it may justify deeper preservation efforts. If not, I suggest we rebind it, document its oddities, and return it to climate-controlled storage with the other

"unclassifiables."

Let someone else decide whether it's madness, metaphor, or something else entirely.

Sincerely,

Dr. Ellory Finch
Hillsather Archivist, Provenance & Rare Materials Division
Department of Special Collections

Postscript V: The Manuscript is Released

From the desk of Benedict Lowre

I did not believe in the manuscript—not in the beginning.

I believed in its potential. In the obscurity. In the madness.

There is currency in madness, you see —especially since it has been unpublished for centuries.

When I first read Vattica Wilde's journal, I dismissed half of it outright. The rest, I curated into coherence, trimming what would be too alarming for a modern audience but leaving in the rot, the dripping rooms, and the whispers in the nursery. Readers like a touch of the grotesque—a soft horror they can distance themselves from—something to flip closed at night.

But Musings of He does not close.

Its final line is not an ending. It is a key.

The publisher insisted on disclaimers and notes from scholars, so I wrote this afterword as a way of grounding the reader again. We are told to tether ourselves to reality in the face of art, as if art is not just another face of reality—one that grins with sharper teeth.

And yet… nothing happened.

No letters from readers speaking of doors coming and going. No sightings of figures cloaked in shadow. No claimed hauntings or whispered dolls. The general response? "Unsettling. Beautifully written. Not for everyone."

Not for everyone.

The ordinary weight of that disappoints me more than I care to admit.

I wanted something. A door left ajar. A voice in the hallway.

But the only thing that has changed— —is me.

There is a sound I cannot place.

A drip. In the quiet hours.

Not rhythmic. Not mechanical.

Wet. Deliberate. Like thought before it becomes a voice.

There are no leaks. No water damage. I've checked.

And yet, it persists.

A slow, hollow drop that seems to echo through the bones of my flat.

There are no visions. No shadows. No dolls.

I sleep as soundly as the average person.

But oddly enough, in my less lucid days, I've begun waking with ink on my hands.

Additions

The following pages were not bound with the rest of the manuscript.

They were discovered folded behind the final board of the journal, loosely wedged between the brittle rear cover and a flattened ribbon—some ink-faded, others nearly torn at the edges. Several were written on different parchments entirely, suggesting they may have been added after the journal's original completion.

There are no dates. No headings. No order to their appearance.

It is impossible to say whether these pages were meant as additions, rewrites, or spontaneous reflections. Some repeat motifs found earlier in the manuscript; others diverge wildly in tone and structure. A few bear bloodstains. One page was found folded into a shape not unlike an envelope but containing nothing within. Another smells faintly of smoke.

I have chosen to include them as they were found: out of sequence, sometimes fragmentary, but unaltered. They seem to me like a final unraveling, a letting go of form.

Whether these scraps are unfinished thoughts or a deliberate final statement, I leave to the reader to decide.

—*Benedict Lowre*

A-I: Addressed to Human Waste

From Vattica Wilde

To Mr. Elbridge Tupp,

Most esteemed Swine, Purveyor of Leaks, Lord of Mold,

The Apartment of 414 Misery Lane,

London (that great slop-hole of a city)

Sir,

Or should I say—Mister, for I will not honour you with the formality of "Sir." That title belongs to men of stature, of dignity, of refined moral compass, and trimmed nose hair. You are not such a man.

Do you hear it? That scratching? That low groan of a pen dragged with glorious ire across the belly of this page? It is the sound of reckoning, Mr. Tupp. It is the sound of judgment made in ink.

I write to you now from a far superior location. A manor, in fact. One with grounds, Mr. Tupp. With corridors and whispers and floorboards that do not scream in protest because someone upstairs cooked an egg. Here, the windows are cracked because of time, not because you patched them with cheap resin and the crushed dreams of other tenants. Here, the mold grows with purpose, not from your refusal to acknowledge basic fungal biology.

But this letter is not to brag. No, I would not lower myself

219

to so petty a gesture.

This letter is vengeance.

Do you recall the leak, Tupp? The one above my writing desk? Of course you do. You pretended not to hear it. You squinted your ratty eyes and said, "Drippin'? I don't hear no drippin'." Oh, how I wanted to drag you to the spot and shove your greasy face into the water spot like one might punish a dog. But dogs are loyal. Dogs have value. You, Mr. Tupp, are more like a... slug that's made peace with its slime.

When I begged for repairs, you offered that half-sniff, half snort of yours, as if my words were nothing but dust to be blown away. And when I stood there—tired, ink-stained, bones cracked from the cold seeping through the floor—you dared to tell me to "just put down a bucket." *A bucket.*

I ask you, does Shakespeare write beside a bucket? Did Milton, blind and brilliant, compose Paradise Lost with a pot to catch the failures of a landlord above him? I think not. You, sir, are the Devil's own property manager.

But let us not linger solely upon the leak. Oh, no.

Let us remember the heating, shall we?

The radiator in my bedroom, that rusted relic of the Crimean War, hissed like a dying snake and gave off less warmth than the breath of a tax collector. I shivered through my work, Tupp. I wrote in gloves. You turned a man of letters into a man of layers. My ink froze mid-sentence. My muse, fragile creature that she is, took one look at the frost on my windows and fled for warmer pastures.

And what of the sounds?

Do you know what it is to hear the ceaseless groaning of a

building that resents your existence? To lie awake as the walls twitch and tremble like a senile beast, moaning from the effort of housing yet another soul? You assured me, "It's just the pipes." I assure you, the pipes whispered my name. The pipes conspired. They gurgled secrets and spite.

And oh, the neighbours. If the building itself was your first crime, then the tenants you curated were your second. On one side: an opera singer who practiced nightly with the warble of a dying loon. On the other hand, a couple who fought like roosters, clucked like hens, and seemed entirely composed of feathers and foul play. Above me, a tap dancer. Or perhaps just a lonely man who wore boots and stomped for company. Below, a silent horror—I never saw them, but I heard their breath through the vents.

You built a zoo and called it a dwelling.

Now, let us speak of rent.

I paid it. Every month. With a groaning wallet and a bleeding conscience, I placed coin and crumpled notes into your claw. And what did you provide? Mold, madness, mildew, and mockery. You treated the building as your inheritance and the tenants as your tenants in hell.

And the day—*the day, Mr. Tupp*—you locked me out, when I returned from the house of God to find my belongings tossed into the hallway like the contents of a woman scorned? Do you recall what I said to you?

No? Then let me remind you.

I said: "This is not the end, Tupp. This is merely the introduction."

Well. Consider this letter the middle act.

The ending shall be written in my triumph.

Do you know where I live now? You do not, and for that I am grateful. But I will tell you this: the house accepts me. It listens.

It breathes. And it has shown me things you cannot fathom. Yes, there is mold, but not yours. This mold is elegant. It is the mold of memory. The kind that grows not from damp ceilings, but from ancient sorrows. You would not understand.

You creature of clogs and coin.

I imagine you still potter down the corridor in your slippers, the ones stained with curry and contempt. Still scratching at your scalp as if lice were your inheritance. Still sniffing about for rent like a pig for truffles. I pity you, in a way. You are bound to that building as a barnacle to a hull. You shall never leave. Not truly.

But I, Vattica Wilde, have ascended.

I write now not for editors but for eternity. Not for rent, but for revelation.

And if the house I occupy whispers, it does so with grace. If it creaks, it sings. If it dreams, it dreams in architecture and blood.

And it has promised me one thing, Tupp.

When the last word is written, when the last ink is spilled, and the final syllable offered, it will send this letter to you—not by post, but by fate. It will crawl through your keyhole and settle beneath your boot. You will read it and know that you failed to break me. That your building, your rot, your miserly meanness- they were the flint, but I was the fire.

Enjoy your dripping.

I now live in the flood.

Most uncordially,

Vattica Wilde
Resident of Hollisby, Writer of Ends, Tenant of the Last Story

A-II: The Pages in the Wall

Amongst painted company

It was the sound again—the dry rustle of something not alive and not quite dead. Not footsteps. Not vermin. Not wind. But something like pages turning where no hands should be.

It led me to the wall in the southern corridor, just beside the warped portrait of a woman with too many fingers. I had passed it countless times before, always distracted by the uneven floorboards or the damp that clung to the air like mildew-slick prayer. But tonight, the air tasted of something else—penny ink, old glue, and bone dust.

A seam had split just beneath the molding—not a full opening, no grand reveal. Just a breath of space. And from it, a single page had curled forward like a claw.

It came out too easily.

Behind it: more.

A narrow cavity stuffed with paper. Hand-bound pages stitched in string, some torn loose and crumpled. All covered in handwriting not my own, but not quite foreign either. The letters slanted differently. A hand perhaps older, or shaking. But the language? The cadence?

It was as if my own thoughts had bled into the margins of another man's mind.

I read. I should not have. But I did.

[Fragmented Page – undated]

He walks the walls behind the plaster. I hear his weight, the slow drag of his robe or coat or skin. He smells of lamp oil and dying fire. He hums, but only when I do not breathe.

[Loose scrap – burned edge]

I was once a poet. Or perhaps a physician. The manor has taken the name from me. I am pages now. Just pages.

[Journal cover – charred, illegible but marked with three dots: ...]

Inside were thirty-seven pages. I counted twice. The first ten bore entries not unlike my own—a man attempting to make sense of the house, of the sounds, of the Him that paced in mirrors and whispered at door hinges. But then the voice shifted.

It grew frantic.

Disjointed.

Then suddenly, fluent again. But not in any human tongue.

I do not mean metaphor. I mean the symbols on the pages changed—twisting glyphs like ink that had learned how to

scream. I stared too long. I admit it. I could not help myself. And then came the last page.

[Final page – written backward, deciphered only by holding it to candlelight]

If you find this, I am still here. I am pressed thin. Between the walls. Beneath the boards. Do not finish your book. He reads it as you write. He binds you to it.

<hr>

I folded the pages carefully, though my hands shook. I thought, for a moment, to burn them. But that felt like complicity. Like feeding Him.

I returned them to the wall. Not out of fear. Out of recognition.

Whoever wrote them was not mad.

He was only further along.

I will sleep in the study tonight.

—V. Wilde

A-III: Dinner and a Show

❦ ❦ ❦

I dined tonight with a man whose name I cannot recall and whose face seemed more a suggestion than a fixture of flesh. Whether he was real or a figment—or perhaps something in between—I cannot say. He came unannounced, stepping into the parlour from a room I had not known connected. He was dressed finely, in a coat of midnight velvet with silver fastenings, and though I cannot remember the details of his features, I know with certainty that he smiled far too much.

He greeted me with unsettling familiarity. "Wilde," he said, as though we had grown up together or shared mistresses. "You dine poorly. You live like a monk in a house meant for kings." I told him I had not invited the company.

"Oh, but company is the marrow of the mind," he replied, seating himself at the empty end of my long dining table. I do not remember lighting the candles, and yet they glowed with a ferocity that made the shadows stretch back as though afraid.

The table was set for two.

Roast pork, thick and steaming, appeared before us—not conjured, not clattered in by servants (for there are none here), but simply present. I know not whether it had been cooked or willed. The smell was nauseating, cloying. It reminded me of the market stalls off Blackfriars Bridge, where butchered meat hangs under fly-blown canvas and stray dogs loiter for scraps.

My guest ate greedily. His teeth were too white. Too even.

And the way he tore at the meat—it made me think of swine.

Between bites, he spoke of mediocrity, of the great herd of men who shuffle through life in service of those more interesting. "Swine and simps," he called them. "The masses, who live as scaffolding for genius. You, Wilde, have been among them too long."

I asked him what he meant.

He leaned forward, his smile never dimming, and said, "You were not made for rejection. You were not made to submit your words like supplicant prayers to philistines in waistcoats. No, you

were made to command. To reign. To become." The word hung in the air.

Become what? He did not say.

The pork on my plate moved.

Not wriggled. Not squirmed.

It breathed.

I looked down and saw, to my horror, that it still bore an eye. Just one. Small and black, like a raisin. It looked at me.

I stood. My chair shrieked against the floorboards. I turned to flee, but the door behind me had vanished. The guest—if guest he was—remained seated, now picking his teeth with a bone. "Don't be rude," he said. "We're only just beginning." I must have fainted. Or escaped. Or dreamed.

I awoke in the study, slumped over the writing desk, my ink bottle spilled, its contents bleeding into the grain like rot. My stomach churns even now. I have eaten nothing since morning, and yet I feel full. Disgustingly, obscenely full.

I dared return to the dining room. It is empty. No pork. No candles. No guest. Only two chairs, askew. And a bone on the table.

Small.

Human.

I have locked every door. I have barred the windows. And still, I feel I am being watched. Not by anything so merciful as ghosts, but by something far older. Far hungrier.

I must write. I must chronicle this descent. Lest I forget myself.

Though truth be told, I no longer know who that self is.

—*V.W.*

A-IV: The Séance

With hands both cold and stuttered

It began with a door that did not exist. Not when I went to sleep, nor when I mapped the hallway the day before, carefully drawing each corner and cornerstone as though the act of naming them would lend me dominion over the house. But there it was, nonetheless: a narrow door of pale ash, half-sunken into the wall near the stairwell landing, as though ashamed to be seen.

In the dream, I opened it.

It led, absurdly, downward—beneath the manor, beneath even the boiler. The staircase was made of stone, slick with condensation, lit only by the faintest bloom of gaslight above. I descended.

The air was thick, like I had stepped inside the breath of a larger creature. The sound of chairs scraping across floorboards echoed faintly from below. At first, I thought I was alone. Then came the whispering.

It began in the drainpipes.

Soft at first, like steam through copper, then sharper, syllabic. Voices—not one, but many—rising and falling in dry chorus. I remember crouching by the rusted pipes that fed down the wall and pressing my ear to them. What I heard, I cannot say for certain. The words were in no tongue I know, but they clung to the inside of my head like old smoke.

I followed the sounds.

At the base of the stairs lay a corridor—narrow, low-ceilinged, lined with portrait frames whose faces had been scratched out. I passed them all with my head bowed—not out of fear, but shame. I had the irrational sensation that I was being watched—not by the portraits, but by the hall itself, as though the walls might blink.

Then: the parlour.

It opened like a wound at the end of the corridor, the door buckling outward as if long denied. I recognised it immediately, though it bore little resemblance to the one I know. The ceiling was higher, the curtains older, the floor somehow... hungrier. Velvet armchairs huddled like conspirators around a small, oaken table. At its center sat a cracked glass bowl and a circle of hands.

Six women. One man. Their faces were indistinct, moving beneath a veil of shadows cast not by candlelight, but by something more internal. The kind of shadow that requires no source.

Yet I saw the details clearly.

The one nearest the bowl had nails like needles. Another wore a necklace of tiny vials, each filled with a trembling fluid the color of bruises. The man had no eyes—just dark, sunken hollows where he seemed to be trying to weep, though nothing fell.

No one spoke. Not aloud.

But the drainpipes did.

They curled along the ceiling like black vines, iron intestines pulsing with speech. I dared not look up. I knew—dream logic knew—that if I did, I would see Him.

And it was Him. Not yet seen. Not yet named. But felt. The way a child feels the shape of a monster in the dark.

They called Him up.

The séance began not with invocation, but with stillness. Each participant bowed their head, and for one terrible moment, I felt them exhale in unison. It filled the room. My lungs seized. It was not air they breathed, but time, or something close to it.

The bowl began to rattle.

Not violently—just enough to suggest the floor no longer belonged to the earth. The curtains pulled inward, toward the table. Chairs creaked not with motion, but with age, as though they had been waiting centuries to be sat in. And then, finally, a voice that was not a whisper:

"He waits for permission." It came from everywhere and nowhere.

The woman with the needle-nails stood. She drew something from her pocket—bone, I think—and laid it in the bowl. One by one, the others followed. A tooth. A key. A fingernail. A paper scrap soaked in something red. When the man reached into his coat, I felt the temperature drop. He placed a shard of mirror, still wet.

They began to chant.

I cannot remember the words, but the rhythm remains in my marrow: three syllables, two, then one—again and again, like a breath falling down a stairwell. The pipes joined them, harmonizing in a language made of teeth and rust. And in that moment, I understood nothing, and everything.

I tried to run.

But the stairwell had vanished.

I was not standing in the hallway. I was not even standing. I was perched halfway up the stairs leading into the parlour— the very stairs I've stood on a dozen times in waking. I was watching the séance from above, as if I had just arrived and dared not interrupt.

They did not see me at first.

The mirror shard cracked.

The woman with the necklace of bruises tilted her head. Her eyes rose toward mine—but not directly. Just above. Just beyond. As though seeing something over my shoulder.

The man followed. His hollows flared with some unseen light. He opened his mouth.

"You are the final guest."

I woke before he spoke again.

There was no scream. No waking sweat. Only the scent of dust, and a slow, shivering certainty that I had witnessed something not entirely unreal.

The parlour remains unchanged in daylight. The furniture is faded, the wallpaper peeling, the chandelier long since broken. The drainpipes are silent. Yet I cannot sit in that room without feeling the pull of a memory that isn't mine.

I have since avoided the stairs after dusk. And I will never touch the pipes.

—V.W.

A-V: Black Pages

Blood in the foyer

There are pages I do not remember writing.

I do not mean the scatterings of thought or the frayed ends of sentences left in haste—no, I mean whole entries. Paragraphs. Poems. Phrases that do not sound like mine and yet bleed with my voice. I discovered them this morning, buried deep within the spine of the journal, after I had attempted to tear out a page I believed had betrayed me.

The page would not tear.

Instead, another fell loose. Black. Entirely black. A sheet of thick parchment drenched in ink, as though a bottle had spilled and the liquid had spread with purpose. Not like a spill at all, in truth—but deliberate. As though the ink had been written not upon the page, but into it. Pressed like a wound.

The ink was raised, like scars. My fingers brushed it and came away stained. That, in itself, would not trouble me. But the ink does not fade.

It's in the grooves of my palms now. Under the nails. Behind the knuckle lines. I have washed and scrubbed and gouged, and nothing lifts it. It has crawled into me, seeped like wine through cloth. My lips feel sticky with it. I spat once, and the saliva was grey.

Worse—my teeth. I see them in the mirror, and they are darkened at the edges, like smoke pressed into enamel.

I turned the page over. There were no words. Not in the way

one expects. But something shimmered when I tilted it. Glossed like oil.

I held it up to the light and saw letters. Tiny, nested within each other, twisting like veins. Not in English. Nor French. Nor Latin. A language I felt rather than read.

And I understood it.

Not intellectually—viscerally. It bypassed my mind and settled into the pit of my chest. A single phrase.

You are no longer the author.

I dropped the page. My knees struck the floor. I retched.

No bile came.

Only black.

The black pages multiply. That's the only word I can think to describe it. Multiply. Like cells. Like mold on bread. I find them tucked between my own entries. I swear they were not there the night before, and yet now they seem anchored in the binding, as though they were always part of the book.

Some are still blank. Others pulse with that raised ink. Some are wet. Actively wet. I placed one on the sill to dry and returned an hour later to find a fly trapped in its center, struggling, its wings fused to the page.

He speaks louder now.

Not in voice. In writing. He is there in the margins of my

thoughts, underlining my madness with glee. I see his hand—long, too long—guiding mine at night. I sleep with ink on my wrists, on the inside of my elbows, my throat. It is a tattoo not meant for the skin. It soaks deeper than memory.

I asked aloud, "What do you want from me?"

And I heard a pen scratch.

That was all.

Not a word. Not a whisper. Just the echo of a sentence forming elsewhere. Perhaps on the next page. Perhaps in the space behind the walls.

I burned one of the pages.

Only one.

It screamed.

I did not imagine it. It gave a high, thin wail like steam escaping a kettle, but thinner, crueler. The sound turned the walls inward. I covered my ears, and still it entered. When the smoke cleared, the page was whole again. No ash. No singe. No burn mark.

Just darker.

So, I tried to trap it.

I placed it in a locked drawer. I shoved the key beneath the floorboards. When I returned, the drawer was empty, and the page was on my desk.

It read:

You will write what is written. Or you will be unwritten.

What can I say to that?

I am a writer. That is my gift. My curse. My inheritance. If He has taken my voice, then I am no longer a man. Just a vessel. Just a pen with bones.

I have not eaten. Not properly. The bread mold is alive. I do not say that metaphorically. It pulses when I reach for it. And the water tastes like paper. I drink it anyway.

Because the ink tastes worse.

Yes—I have tasted it. He made me.

Today, the black pages were waiting on the floor. Laid out like stepping stones. A trail that led me from my bed to the study. I did not follow. My legs refused. But the room began to stretch until I had no choice.

Each step left my feet darker. Stained. And with each step, a memory surfaced.

414.

The gloves.

The mouth that whispered "You are loved" in a voice that smelled like salt and copper.

I have tried to forget that night. That boy. That thing that was not yet me. But the ink knows. It remembers what I buried. And now, it writes it back into me. One page bore the words:

He lies about what he saw in the river. He knows what floated by.

I do not. I swear it. I only know the sound. The gurgling. The way the reeds split. The gasp of something rising.

And Étienne screaming.

I do not remember the face. Only the hand. Wet and white and pointing at me.

There was a new page this evening. It was nailed to the ceiling.

Yes. Nailed.

A perfect, black square, pinned by rusted nails, I do not remember placing. I fetched a chair to remove it, and when I stood atop it, I saw the words upside down.

Your eyes are borrowed.

And then my vision blurred. I blinked—and saw another room.

The nursery.

But not as it is now. As it was. Before the rot. Before the silence. There were toys. Laughter. A crib with the name Vattica scrawled into its side.

I fell from the chair.

When I came to, the page was gone. But my hand bore the same words. Etched into my palm in mirror ink.

I tried to scrub it off.

The skin peeled.

The words did not.

He is writing through me.

That is the truth I feared, but now accept.

He uses my hand at night. He speaks through my thoughts. The stories are no longer mine. I find tales written that I do not remember inventing. Some are vile. Some are beautiful in ways that make me weep. But none are mine.

I saw myself today—in the mirror. But the reflection was writing.

I was not.

It looked up and smiled.

I did not.

There is one page left.

I know it's the last because it glows.

Faintly. From within. Not light, not heat. Just the sense of ending.

I have not read it.

I am afraid that if I do, I will cease.

I will sit in silence now.

And wait.

For the ink to finish me.

A-VI: The Letter Not Sent

(Recovered from a sealed envelope found within the lining of Vattica Wilde's manuscript case. Ink faded. Handwriting increasingly unstable. The original text was reversed, as if it were meant only for mirrors or memory.)

--- ❦ ❦ ❦ ---

He has bled backwards.

He has bled backwards.

He has bled backwards

He had bled backwards.

—I cannot keep the ink from weeping. Even the quill shivers. I tried to write to you all plainly, but grief has syntax, and it twists every phrase into an elegy.

Forgive me for wasting the life you so desperately fought for.

It should have been me.

You were the gold.

The ink bled through my fingertips. The page swallowed my voice. I do not know if these words are legible anymore, or if they simply echo.

Have I lost to the madness of my own wiles?

Have I forgotten my sins? Why does He remember?

Why was He watching?

—I remember your laughter most of all. It arrived like bells through the fog. But memory is brittle parchment, and time is ash.

If I am folly at least I am interesting.

If I am broken, at least I am alive.

Sing.

Sing his praises.

—They will say I was lost to madness. Let them. I only ever wanted to open a door they kept sealed.

He speaks in allegory.

I fear my thoughts are no longer my own.

I fear sanctuary has lost me.

—My hands no longer obey me. This letter is not written—it is spilled.

I merely wanted to be seen.

I wanted your voice to be heard.

Now I do not remember.

My story is gone.

—Each line comes heavier than the last. Not with weight, but with returning. Like breath that's already been drawn and exhaled a hundred times by mouths not mine.

Blame me.

Blame me for the sin of wanting cake with pink frost-

—I've dreamt of each of you, faceless, voiceless, and yet known to me by silence alone. Silence is how He names things.

It is too loud in the corridor.

The stories do not end.

They merely wait until they are hungry again.

—I left the door open, not to escape, but to allow you a way in—should you ever need to find me beneath what remains.

I believe I made a grave mistake.

—I am not gone. Only translated. One can live backward through scripture if one's tongue remembers its source.

He remembers in reverse.

He remembers in reverse.

He remembered in reverse.

—You who held my name in trust: it will not vanish. Speak it once more, not with lips, but with grief. Let it echo.

I cannot sleep.

I wake up at the desk with quill in hand.

The manuscript does not sleep.

—He listens. He always has. That was the lesson written in fire, beneath the ink: to write is to resurrect Him.

Was he always here?

Or did I breathe life into my insolence?

—I burned the pages with my own name on them. Even now, I am uncertain whether it was an erasure or a plea.

I can taste the rot. I heard God sneer.

—I remembered your voices. They kept me from vanishing entirely. Grief anchored me when ink could not.

Forgive me for being the last to hear you.

Forgive me for letting the current lake your hand from mine.

I write with sin.

—Still, I could not call back what was taken. The silence I carry now is not peace. It is an inheritance.

247

I plagiarized you.

I glorified your hell.

—To each of you, I give this: not closure, but a warning. The story never ends. It only unwrites.

I remember names from faces long lost.

Do you?

Or have you lost your way as well?

—Hold no shrine for me. Only pages. If you must weep, do it onto paper. Let your grief be a gospel unbound.

You suffered for my greatness.

Let my suffering be your offerings.

—I am not healed. I am not holy. I am merely remembered.

Even God cannot stave this ego.

—If you find this, it means I have lingered too long. If you read it, then I was never truly alone.

Lay me bare the way I laid myself in beds through cold.

May the creature I've become haunt those need so. I hold no regrets in this moment. I hold greatness.

As I have always deserved. As I have always been.

—*Vattica Wilde*

A-VII: Written to the Loathed

Mother, Father,

It seems absurd, doesn't it? To write to you now. To sit in this quiet, isolated place and imagine that either of you could ever receive these words. I am an adult now, and yet here I am, clutching my pen like the small boy I once was—grieving not just for you, but for the ghosts you left behind. I never did much to earn your love, did I? But that's beside the point. You did nothing to earn my forgiveness, either.

You were never there. Neither of you.

I write to you both now, though I do not know where either of you is—if anywhere at all. You may have left this world years ago, but you still haunt me. Your absence, like your presence, clings to me, suffocating every attempt to free myself. I spent so many years thinking I could outrun the weight of you both, but I find now that there is nowhere to go. You live in me still, lurking, twisting my thoughts like parasites.

I do not know how I have come to this point, where my heart aches so deeply for those who could never care for me. Yet, here I sit, writing to you as though you were ever truly capable of understanding me.

Do you know what I've discovered, Mother? Do you know what I've realized only now, after all these years of muddled thoughts and repressed memories? You were a woman of no consequence. You were never *my* mother. I do not know if you ever knew the meaning of the word.

You died in a brothel, didn't you? Not that I should be

surprised. The world had already marked you long before your body gave out. My memories of you are nothing more than faint images of your shadowed face as you lay in the grimy bed, the smell of stale perfume clinging to you like a shroud. What else is there to remember? The times you laid your hands on me— always so cold, always so detached. Never warm, never caring. You made me feel like I was an inconvenience. A mistake, something that didn't belong.

And Father... *Father*... You were nothing. I know little about you. Nothing of substance. What I do know, I was told. The men who lingered in the dark corners of the brothels whispered about you. So many stories, all the same. You were nothing more than a broken man, a low, worthless thing who could not even bother to stay around. I heard you were a drunk, that you spent your days with whores and your nights drowning in the deepest part of your shame.

And yet, for all the loathing I feel for you—*for all the contempt I hold for your memory*—I still find myself wondering, deep down, if you were better than I thought. You see, Father, I always thought you the worst man imaginable. But in truth, I don't know what you looked like, what you sounded like. I don't know anything. You were a shadow, a myth. All I know is the echo of your name, a name that was never more than a mockery.

I suppose that's the way you wanted it. You never left anything behind. No legacy, no trace. *Nothing*.

But then there's Étienne.

God, Étienne. What a boy. I adored him. He was my only link to something pure, something that could make sense of all this nonsense. He was always so beautiful, so full of life. He carried none of my burdens. Not like I did. *I* was the one who was burdened by you two. But Étienne, he was your salvation, wasn't he, Mother? You carried him inside you like a prized possession.

You must have known what he was worth.

But did you ever realize, Mother? Did you ever see the distinction between him and me? You never once told me about Étienne's father. Never once did you speak of him. But I have my own thoughts on the matter, drawn from the whispers I heard— both real and imagined. There was something *different* about Étienne. Something I couldn't put into words, not until now. He wasn't born from the same filth you brought me into. I can only imagine that his father was a man of stature, someone of *worth*. A man who could afford to have a son who wasn't *me*.

Was he a lord? A man of wealth and taste, perhaps? A man who could afford to lavish gifts upon you, a man whose blood ran pure and untainted. He must have been, for you to treat Étienne like some kind of *royalty* while I was cast aside, left to the streets with nothing but the filth of your mistakes.

I hated you for it, Mother. I hated you for giving him the life I could never have. It was as if you had betrayed me. It was as if you had *chosen* him.

He was *everything* I was not.

And yet, I loved him. I loved him like a brother should be loved. He was my only family, my only real companion. He didn't deserve the fate you gave him. This fate of being *ours*, of being born into that same madness.

I wish he were here with me now. I wish he could have known what I know. Perhaps then, he might have understood why I had to come here. To this place. To *Hollisby*. You wouldn't understand, Mother. You wouldn't care. But Étienne would have.

I keep him with me in the form of memory. His face, so

clear in my mind. His laugh, his smile. He was my redemption, my hope. But now, even that is fading. He's gone, and I am left with only myself. Only the remnants of a broken lineage.

If you could have seen it- if you could have seen me now. You'd be proud of me, wouldn't you? You'd finally see that I was more than just your mistake. But I don't care. It doesn't matter anymore. The world can think of me as they please, as they always have. The pages of this manuscript will remain my legacy, not your hollow gestures.

I'll write for Étienne.

I'll write so he knows I loved him.

And I'll write so I can forget you both.

—*Vattica*

A-VIII: A Letter to My Brother

My dearest Étienne,

I have found it again＿the urge to write to you. A compulsion more than a desire. A soft scratching that begins behind my eyes and moves into my hands, until the ink must spill somewhere, or I think I shall bleed it instead. I know you will not receive this letter. I know there is no post that delivers to the dead. But still, I write. If only I could return to a version of myself that once believed in you. In us.

They say madness is a spiral, but I have come to believe it is a mirror. One sees only oneself, again and again, until the image fractures. I do not know what I see now. I know only that your name remains the single syllable I can still write without shame.

I remember you in pieces. A wrist, a scarf, the way your jaw tensed when you lied. That last part I remember best. Because you were always the better liar. And I? I was always the better fool.

Do you recall the attic in Paris, that foul-smelling garret with its sloped ceiling and the window that never closed properly? We used to laugh at the wind, saying it was a ghost that crept in to pull our blankets off at night. You used to say, "Let it come in. It keeps the air from going stale." And I believed you, as I always did. I think, in some way, I miss that wind most of all.

Do you remember how we used to sleep curled together in that broken bed? We were not yet men, though the city insisted we play the part. And you—so clever with your hands and your

255

thieving fingers—you made it a game. Always a game. You'd return with coins still warm from another man's pocket and smile as if you had just won us the moon.

And I? I was the one who warmed the beds. Who was passed from hand to hand like a soft-wrapped sweet. I hated them, Étienne. I hated their eyes and their breath and their trembling mouths that said such gentle things in the dark. And yet—I smiled. Because that was what you needed, and I would have burned down the world for you.

But you left me.

You left me beneath the golden arches of that bridge, with the sky cracked open and the river swollen like a bloated tongue. Your fingers slipped from mine in silence. No dramatic farewell. No confession of love or regret. Just the slick rush of your weight vanishing into the Seine. You didn't even look back.

They found your shoe three days later. One shoe. And nothing else.

I told myself you had run—that you had finally taken the money and escaped to Marseille, or perhaps the coast. That you were alive somewhere, sipping wine and laughing. But I knew. I *knew*. You would never have gone without me.

So, I wrote The Brothers of Gold. Do you remember? Of course you do. Everyone remembers. It was the only time the world listened when I spoke. I told our story, though I softened the truth. They could not stomach our hunger. Our filth. They could not bear the rawness of what we were. So, I polished it. I made us tragic and beautiful, as if poetry could mask the stench of the gutters we slept in. And they wept. They wept and called me a genius.

But it was your blood I wrote with. They do not know that.

They do not understand that every line in that book was a scream I had swallowed.

They called me a wunderkind. A prodigy. As if I had birthed that story from my soul rather than carved it from your corpse. I should have buried it with you. Instead, I gilded it and sold it.

Now look at me. A man alone in a crumbling manor, scribbling letters to ghosts and feeding on ink. The floorboards groan with secrets. The walls shift when I sleep. There is a voice that speaks in riddles, always from the corner of my eye. And still—I write.

I have rewritten the novel, you know. Not to be published. No, not for them. For you. For me. For the truth. It is not called The Brothers of Gold anymore. It is something else. Something darker. Something truer. The Brothers of Mold, I've titled it. Because that is what we were, wasn't it? Mold growing between the bricks of a crumbling city. You, the brilliant spore. Me, the rot that clung to your heel.

Do you hate me, Étienne?

Do you hate that I lived?

I would understand if you did.

There are days I look into the mirror and see your mouth forming my words. Days I wake to the weight of your arm over my chest and realize it is only a dream—or worse, a memory I invented to keep from unraveling.

There is a doll in this house. One eye. One perfect, unblinking eye. I think of you when I see it. I think of how you used to cover my eyes before I wept, and how you'd hum to drown out the sounds outside our door. I think of your voice the night before you died. "You'll be a writer," you said. "Better than any of them. Even the ones with names in marble." And I laughed because I was cold and hungry and too tired to believe in anything.

You made me promise to write us into eternity. And I did.

But I left out the worst parts. The things I didn't want anyone to know. The men. The silk gloves. The blood that was never mine.

I remember something now. Something I had buried.

You killed someone, didn't you?

That man with the black coat and the red-lined sleeves. The one who liked to watch. I remember his teeth. I remember how he bled. And I remember your face—not afraid, not angry. Just still. Perfectly still.

We ran, of course. You told me not to speak of it again. And I didn't. Not to anyone. Not even to myself.

Until now.

I wonder if that was the moment we ceased to be brothers and became something else—something darker, something bound in silence.

And now, I hear footsteps behind the walls. A voice murmuring stories only I can write. I do not know if it is you. Or Him. Or some echo of myself that has learned how to haunt the spaces I abandoned.

But I miss you.

I miss the weight of your hand in mine, the shared heat of hunger, and the language of glances that meant the difference between life and death.

If there is a heaven, you are not in it. We were not made for such places. If there is a hell, I suspect I have already begun to live in its vestibule. But if there is something else—some in-between place of ash and ink and memory—then I hope you read this.

And if you do… please forgive me.

Not for living. But for how poorly I have done it.

I will see you again.

Soon, I think.

He tells me so.

Your brother,
Always,
Vattica

A-IX: A Letter While You Sleep

[Editor's Note: The following was found tucked deep within the inner pocket lining of the journal, folded far more gently than the other loose-leaves and written entirely in pencil. Much of the words were worn by time, but careful deciphering has allowed it to be transcribed.]

Mon frère,

I write this with little candle, the wax drip on my fingers as I do. You are sleeping beside me. I can hear your breath. It makes clouds in the cold air, like little ghosts from your lips. You always say I must not waste paper, but this one I stole just for you. I saw you today, shaking. You say it is only cold but I know it is more than that. Je sais que tu as mal. Je sais que la rue n'est pas faite pour toi.

But you still walk it. Every night. You stand in the places with the yellow lamps and the men with long coats. You talk to women with teeth like broken glass. You wait for the drunk ones. I see them. I hate them. I want to make them disappear for you.

I want you to never stand there again.

Je promets, Vattica. Je promets que nous allons partir d'ici. I will make enough. I will take coin from every drunk fool in Montmartre. I will pick pockets like magic. You always say I have the fingers for it. Long and light like a cat. I will take from all the fat ones who drink too much and laugh too loud and touch girls who don't smile back.

I will take and take until we have enough for train tickets.

Enough for bread. For coats with lining. For *boots*, Vattica.

Imagine that—your own boots! Not ones with holes. Ones that are quiet when you walk.

London is real. You told me so. I heard it in your stories. "Across the water," you say. "A place where even the fog wears a crown." You said they don't spit on you there if your coat is old. That they pay men who write. That they have libraries with real fires and chairs you can fall asleep in.

Je veux y aller. Je veux que toi et moi on soit des Anglais. De vrais Anglais. Avec des cravates et des livres et pas de peur.

You are the smartest boy in all of Paris. I know it. You know more words than the priests and more ideas than the painters. I've seen you write in your little book even when your hands shake too much to hold a pencil. I've seen the way your face looks when you make up a sentence so beautiful you forget to breathe.

You could write a book that makes kings cry.

And me—I could sell them. Stand in the street and shout your name like you were Victor Hugo. You said Hugo wasn't even handsome. That you are prettier than any man who ever wrote a word. I think so too.

When we get to London, I'll stop stealing. I'll stop everything. I'll wear a real shirt and tuck it in. I'll learn how to say the words right, not like this, not in broken mouth like now. I'll be proper. I'll find us a room with two beds. Or maybe bunk beds! You on top because you are the oldest. I don't care if you get mad that I snore. I will.

I'll find a job and you'll write and we'll be real people. Not shadows.

Tu seras libre, Vattica. Libre de la saleté, du froid, des coins sombres où tu dois te cacher. Libre des hommes aux yeux morts. Je te vois après que tu les as quittés. Ton dos se courbe, tes épaules tombent. Tu es triste même quand tu souris. Je veux que tu souries pour de vrai.

You always try to hide it, but I hear you cry sometimes. When you think I sleep. I don't say nothing because I know you'd get angry. But I do hear. And it makes something in me scream. I want to be big enough to fight for you. But I'm not big. Not yet.

One day I will be.

And when I am, I'll carry you away from here if I have to. I'll carry you like a knight. Not on a horse. We can't afford a horse. But maybe a train. Or a cart. Or just my legs.

Vattica… tu es tout ce que j'ai. Tu es mon frère, mais aussi mon maman, mon papa, mon maison. Tu es ma famille entière. Tu es la voix qui me lit les livres même quand t'as pas mangé. Tu es les mains qui me couvrent quand j'ai froid. Tu es le cœur que je n'ai pas encore compris.

Je veux que tu vives.

I want that more than I want bread.

You said once that some people are born from stars. I think you are one. A fallen star, landed in the dirt. I want to clean the dirt off. I want the world to see how you shine.

I know people say we are nothing. Bastards. Street filth. Boys without a future. I hear them. I know what they mean when they say *boys like us*. But I don't believe them. I believe you. I believe your stories. I believe in London and the fog and the ink that never dries.

I'll be the boy who gets us there.

Je volerai mille fois s'il le faut. Je couperai la main de celui qui te touche sans ton accord. Je mentirai, je tricherai, je courrai toute la ville pour toi.

And when we're there—when we've made it—we'll go to the biggest bakery and buy the stupidest cake. Pink frosting. Too much sugar. We'll eat until we feel sick and then laugh until we cry. You'll have a quill made of real bird feather. I'll buy it for you. You'll write your stories and I'll tell everyone: *That's my brother. The one who made the whole world out of nothing.*

But until then, I'll keep stealing. I'll keep running. I'll keep fighting. So you don't have to.

Sleep tonight, Vattica. Just sleep. Je te protégerai, même en rêve.

—*Étienne*
(your little shadow, your stupid brother who loves you so much it hurts)

Qu'il repose là où les mots ne suivent plus.

Words from the Author

First and foremost, thank YOU. Thank you for picking up this book. Thank you for reading it. And thank you for caring enough to read this.

Thank you for following Vattica's journey and for making the dreams of one dumb girl with a laptop and a brain buzzing with ideas come true. I've been writing stories since middle school, starting with a high fantasy series that will NEVER see the light of day. So I have the greatest gratitude to you, the reader, who saw this book and decided the pages were worth flipping through.

Secondly, an enormous thank you to Vattica himself. Yes, my mentally ill little man. I mean it when I say he got me off the bathroom floor. I was swamped with school, severely depressed, and going through a crisis that resulted in me having a full-on sobbing breakdown on my bathroom floor. I hated everything I wrote and just happened to remember a story I had been brainstorming, and that's when I heard his voice. In my own head, of course, but it was like he was in the bathroom with me. Telling me that if I'm going to lose my mind, at least do it on paper.

So, I did. And it was the greatest decision I had ever made.

So an enormous thank you to him, for being louder than the noise.

And an enormous thank you to Him, for being louder than the silence.

And finally, a thank you to Hermes, who this book is truly for.

PHEW! I won't lie; this was probably the biggest task I've ever undertaken. I've had The Musings of He rattling around in my head for quite a few years, and honestly it almost went unwritten. I tend to hyper fixate on a story, get a new idea, then lose interest in the original concept. But Vattica kinda kicked me in the pants and said write my story NOW. He's quite bossy like that. But it was needed and I don't regret it one bit.

This story went through A LOT. I spent every last dime I had on it and considered submitting it to be published traditionally but quite frankly I don't think it's the type of story a traditional published would care too much for and I was worried it wouldn't be loved as creatively as I love it. Plus, I had already come up with too much lore for Hillsather and I they're my biggest motivation for writing (there's already a new story in the works).

Hillsather started as a fun little fake publishing house to give the "manuscript" some validity, but I started getting really attached to how their publishing style works. I came up with a whole personality for Benedict Lowre, started thinking about his colleagues and what kind of works they'd publish. A tiny detail of The Musings of He became the driving force for my writing and a creative outlet. It keeps my pen moving and my fingers typing.

I think the hardest part of creating this book wasn't the writing, that honestly came pretty easy thanks to Vattica's voice. But it was doing everything essentially all on my own. While Hillsather in its lore is a large, dedicated team of curators, researchers, editors, archivists, and designers, in reality I am but one girl. I did the cover—which started with a paid cover that I truthfully did not like and just remade myself, found beta readers, paid for editors, formatted all on my own, and somehow got this book into your hands. It's the biggest project I've ever taken on, and I think I lost more money than necessary dealing with scammers and unprofessionalism, but eventually, I found my groove.

I think my biggest fear in writing this story was my very very heavy use of the em dash. In our literary age, AI books are on the RISE and I was terrified my work would be thrown in with the "that's AI written because of the em dashes!" bowl. But I kinda learned that no matter how you write, if you write well people will think that anyways. So just write. Write what you love. Write what makes you feel. And most importantly, write authentically. People can tell when a story has a soul.

I think I've rambled on long enough, so once again, THANK YOU. From the bottom of my silly little heart, thank you. And I hope to meet you again at the next Hillsather story.

Ink stains.
Memories linger.
Hillsather publishes both

.

—*Elowen Greywell*